THE BULLET
AND THE BOMB

Pike Cutler stomped onto the landing and started down. At the sight of Skye Fargo he stopped. "You!" he snarled, hefting a wooden keg clasped in his enormous paws. "It's all your doing. When I'm done with those savages, I'll deal with you." His features were a twisted perversion of anything human, his eyes wide, the pupils dilated. "This will do the job!" He lifted the keg higher, revealing a fuse that jutted from the top.

Fargo's Colt boomed.

Jarred onto his heels, Pike Cutler swayed but did not fall. He hissed defiantly. His left hand moved and a match flared brightly. "Think that will stop me?" he railed.

Again Fargo worked the hammer, and a fourth time. Each shot staggered the man mountain. Yet Cutler's iron will propelled him down the stairs, one lumbering step at a time. The match touched the tip of the fuse, which spat sparks and hissed like a venomous serpent. Spinning, Fargo sprinted toward the entrance.

Mocking laughter echoed off the walls. . . .

THE
TRAILSMAN
#197

UTAH
UPRISING

by

Jon Sharpe

A SIGNET BOOK

SIGNET
Published by the Penguin Group
Penguin Putnam Inc., 375 Hudson Street,
New York, New York 10014, U.S.A.
Penguin Books Ltd, 27 Wrights Lane,
London W8 5TZ, England
Penguin Books Australia Ltd,
Ringwood, Victoria, Australia
Penguin Books Canada Ltd, 10 Alcorn Avenue,
Toronto, Ontario, Canada M4V 3B2
Penguin Books (N.Z.) Ltd, 182–190 Wairau Road,
Auckland 10, New Zealand

Penguin Books Ltd, Registered Offices:
Harmondsworth, Middlesex, England

First published by Signet, an imprint of Dutton Signet,
a member of Penguin Putnam Inc.

First Printing, May, 1998
10 9 8 7 6 5 4 3 2 1

The Trailsman

Beginnings . . . they bend the tree and they mark the man. Skye Fargo was born when he was eighteen. Terror was his midwife, vengeance his first cry. Killing spawned Skye Fargo, ruthless, cold-blooded murder. Out of the acrid smoke of gunpowder still hanging in the air, he rose, cried out a promise never forgotten.

The Trailsman they began to call him all across the West: searcher, scout, hunter, the man who could see where others only looked, his skills for hire but not his soul, the man who lived each day to the fullest, yet trailed each tomorrow. Skye Fargo, the Trailsman, and the seeker who could take the wildness of a land and the wanting of a woman and make them his own.

1861,
southern Utah, where one man's lust
for power swept innocents up in a
whirlwind of bloodshed and slaughter . . .

1

The wilderness was full of surprises.

Skye Fargo had been traveling through some of the most rugged country west of the Mississippi for the better part of a week. After leaving Salt Lake City he had skirted the eastern edge of the Great Salt Lake Desert, an inferno unfit for man or beast. Once past the Sevier Plateau he had followed the Sevier River to the southeast, with majestic Mount Dutton rearing over ten thousand feet high on his left. Now he was in a spectacular region made up of rough, broad uplands slashed by deep canyons and isolated valleys, a region few white men ever visited.

So it was all the more puzzling to scale a ridge and see in the center of a low plain below a couple of buildings and a corral. Wisps of smoke curled lazily from a chimney and several dogs romped nearby.

Fargo's steely lake blue eyes narrowed. His brow knit. A big, broad-shouldered man, he sat the saddle as someone born to it, his muscular buckskin-clad frame hinting at the raw power in his limbs. Resting a hand on the Colt on his right hip, he reined down the ridge and across the dry plain. Overhead a hawk wheeled, inspecting him, then it screeched and soared off in search of prey.

The dogs stopped frolicking to watch his approach, their tails erect, their ears pricked. As he drew closer they moved to intercept his pinto stallion. Tongues lolling, teeth glistening in the bright sunlight, they planted themselves just past the corral and regarded him with open menace. As he came within earshot the dog in the middle growled. They were big brutes, sturdy mongrels with dark glittering eyes, the kind that could hold their own against a pack of wolves.

Fargo wrapped his palm around the Colt. He had dealt with vicious dogs before and knew that if they attacked they would go for the Ovaro's legs to bring the horse down. To show fear, to hesitate, invited a rush. Locking his gaze on the big leader, Fargo rode straight for them. He was well aware of the belief held by most mountain men that animals could be cowed by a human stare. It had been his experience that nine times out of ten the ruse worked, although exactly why was anybody's guess. Some claimed it was because the Almighty intended for man to be the masters of the beasts. Others felt it was due to the fact that a cold, hard stare was the mark of a fierce predator.

Whatever the reason, it worked again. The three mongrels slowly backed off, rumbling in their barrel chests, the leader snapping at empty air as if eager to grind his fangs on Fargo's bones. They retreated past the corral when suddenly the big one crouched and dug his claws into the ground, girding for a charge. Just then a woman cried out, "Fang, no!" From out of a ramshackle stable came a lithe Indian maiden who boldly marched up to the dogs and kicked one of them in the rump. All three backed off, but they were not happy about it.

Fargo's interest switched to his benefactor. She was young and lovely, her lush figure covered by a soft fawn skin dress decorated with beads at the shoulders and neck. Raven hair, clipped short, was bound by a leather headband. Frank eyes regarded him with equal interest, and when he smiled in greeting she offered a shy grin in return. Cradled in her left arm was a bowl containing half a dozen eggs. "Thanks for lending a hand," he said. "I'd hate to have to shoot one of your dogs."

The woman bestowed a look on the trio that told Fargo she would not have minded one bit. "Fang, Slash, and Ripper are not mine," she answered in near-flawless English. Her voice was a throaty purr, and it sent a sensual tingle down the Trailsman's spine.

"Who do they belong to, then?"

From a porch attached to the second building a man answered. "They're mine, stranger. And if you get off that pinto of yours before I say you can, they'll eat you for dinner."

Fargo swiveled. The other building was as poorly built as the stable, but this one had a large sign over the porch that proclaimed to the whole world in crudely painted letters that it was CORNCOB BOB'S TRADING POST. Leaning on a spindly rail was a portly man in grimy clothes, who had an unlit corncob pipe jutting from the corner of his mouth. "Corncob Bob, I take it," Fargo said dryly.

"You reckon right, mister," declared the proprietor as he walked around the rail and stepped down. Out of the trading post ambled two more men, both as grubby as Corncob Bob. Human coyotes, if ever Fargo had seen any. The foremost was a tall drink of water who wore a Remington, butt forward on his left side. The second man, a small ratty specimen whose thin mustache resembled whiskers, sported a pair of Smith & Wesson revolvers in a wide belt adorned with silver studs. "Now suppose you tell me who you are and what you're doing here?"

Fargo turned the Ovaro so he was facing them. "Maybe you haven't heard, friend. But it's not considered polite in these parts to stick your nose into someone else's business."

Corncob Bob did not have a weapon that Fargo could see. Placing his pudgy hands on his ample stomach, he tilted his head to study Fargo a moment, then said amiably enough, "Don't get your hackles up, stranger. A man can't be too careful, is all. This territory is chock full of hardcases and badmen. For all I know, you could be out to rob me."

The two gunmen, Fargo noticed, had not left the porch. They stood in the shadows, their thumbs hooked in their gunbelts, acting casual as could be but fooling no one. "All I'm interested in is some coffin varnish and a meal." He nodded at the stable. "And maybe some feed for my horse if you've got any to spare."

"I'm plumb out of oats but there's plenty of hay," Corncob Bob said. "Help yourself to a stall. The pitchfork is in the front corner." His flat gray eyes roved over the stallion, lingering on the saddle and the stock of the Henry that poked out from the long scabbard. "That's a fine rig you've got there. Been on the go a far piece to judge by all that dust."

"That I have," Fargo admitted. "And I never figured on finding a trading post way out here. Who do you get for customers? The Indians?"

The question must have reminded Corncob Bob of the maiden bearing the eggs. Turning toward her, he snapped, "What the hell are you doing just standing there, you lazy cuss? Didn't I give you a bunch of chores to do?" He raised a hand as if to slap her and she meekly bowed her head, making no effort to protect herself.

"I am sorry. But the dogs were about to attack this man."

"So you took it on yourself to interfere?" Corncob Bob grabbed her by the arm and shoved her toward the porch. "From now on just do as I tell you and let me worry about my dogs." He added a few oaths, then sighed and said to Fargo, "Damn squaw is more trouble than she's worth. It's all that education. She learned our tongue from a Bible thumper, and now she thinks we should treat her as an equal. Can you imagine that?"

Skye Fargo did not respond. Inside of him an icy knot had formed. He saw the two gunmen leer at the woman as she scurried inside. The ratlike man even had the gall to take a swipe at her backside, but she was too quick for him.

"As for the meal you're wanting," Corncob Bob had gone on, "I can have Sue whip up some eggs and venison. And to wash it down I'll treat you to some of the best sipping whiskey ever made. How would that be?"

"Just fine." Fargo reined the pinto to the left and entered the gloomy interior of the stable. It only held six stalls, four of which were filled. At the rear were about twenty chickens, clucking and pecking the ground or nestled snugly in cubbyholes set up for them to lay their eggs. A rooster sat on a bench, preening. A few yards from the bench was a small pen containing five noisy pigs. The place reeked of odors that would gag a member of polite society.

After stripping his saddle off, Fargo located the pitchfork and thrust it into a sizeable pile of hay. Soon he had heaped enough in front of the stallion. With his rifle tucked under an arm, he strolled to the trading post. The three dogs were by the corral, and not once did they take their eyes off him. No one was outside. Pausing at the steps, he scanned the stark mesas to the southeast and the Paunsagunt Plateau to the southwest. There was not another sign of human habitation anywhere.

The inside of the post was almost as dim as the stable. On the right a counter ran the length of the wall, on the left were two tables. The trade goods, such as they were, had been thrown into a single corner, blankets and pots and trinkets all jumbled together. Fargo took a seat, placing his chair so his back was to the wall and he could command a view of the entire room. He set his rifle on the table within easy reach.

Corncob Bob was behind the counter. The two gunmen were at the far end, drinking. Of the woman there was no sign, although faint sounds issued from a doorway at the rear. Fargo pushed the brim of his hat back and ran a hand over his chin. He wouldn't mind a bath, but from the looks of the owner, Corncob Bob had never used a tub in his life and wasn't likely to have one on the premises.

Through the doorway hustled the maiden, her chin tucked to her chest, her hands folded at her waist. She had the air of a frightened doe. Avoiding the two gunmen, she came to Fargo's table. "Pardon me. But how would you like your eggs and steak?" she timidly asked, while out of the corner of her eyes she peeked at the counter where Corncob Bob was treating himself to a drink right from the bottle.

"You're Sue?" Fargo said. He had assumed the trader referred to a white woman, possibly his wife.

"It is the name he has given me," the maiden said, jabbing a slender finger at the slovenly figure. "He finds it too hard to say my real one."

"What is it?"

Before the woman could reply, Corncob Bob smacked the whiskey bottle onto the counter and bellowed. "What's all the jabbering, girl? Just find out what he wants and fix it. And don't dally, if you know what's good for you."

Terror flared in the maiden's eyes, genuine, unbridled fear so potent she blanched and nervously wrung her fingers. Fargo was going to ask why she was so scared but he did not want the trader to grow any madder at her than he already was. Besides, for all Fargo knew, Sue *was* the man's wife. Maybe not in a strictly legal sense, with a swapping of vows and a ring. But many a frontiersman had taken up with an Indian woman, sometimes out of love, more often out of lust. It was a sad fact that quite a few tribes allowed their maidens to be bartered for, or outright bought. "Scrambled eggs and a rare steak will do," he told her.

Nodding, she scampered off. But as she passed the two gunmen, the rat-faced man's hand flicked out faster than the darting tongue of a snake and closed on her wrist, jerking her up short.

"What's your rush, darlin'? Why don't you let Rufus and me treat you to some firewater?"

"I have a meal to cook," Sue said and tried to pull her arm loose, but the gunman would not let go.

"It can wait."

"Please, Mr. Lafferty. You're hurting me." The woman took a step back and wrenched mightily but only succeeded in causing herself more pain. She glanced at Corncob Bob in mute appeal. All he did was tip the bottle and gulp great mouthfuls, half the whiskey spilling over his fleshy jowls and trickling down his thick neck.

"What's wrong with a little pain, sweetheart?" Lafferty said with relish. "It's more fun that way." Shifting, he pulled her against him and held her close. She thrashed and wriggled, becoming more and more desperate, to no avail.

Corncob Bob lowered the bottle and belched. "Lafferty, you know the rules. You can't manhandle the squaw like that. Fork over five dollars first or go out to the stable and fondle that ornery mare of yours."

Rufus had reached up to run his fingers through the maiden's hair. "It's been a coon's age since I had me a female. How about both of us at once, Bob? How much would that come to?"

"Can't you add? Ten dollars."

"We should get a discount," Rufus said. "Be a nice guy and shave some off since we're good pards and all. I've only got two dollars on me, plus some change. I suppose I could throw in my watch, even though it's busted."

Corncob Bob moved down the counter. "This ain't no charity, you peckerwood. What in the world would I do with a broken watch? I don't ever care what time it is." Extending his left palm, he wagged it under their noses. "Ten dollars, you two, and that's final. Don't raise a fuss, either, or Pike will hear of it."

The men were so intent on haggling that none of them paid any attention to Fargo. Rising with the Henry in his left hand, he wound past the tables and around a stack of blankets and other merchandise, coming up on the gunmen from the rear. The maiden was still striving to free herself from Lafferty's grasp and happened to see him. Her eyes widened when she saw his expression and she shook her head as if to warn him off. But Fargo did not heed. Planting himself squarely, he declared, "Mind if I have a say?"

Lafferty and Rufus both turned, neither anticipating trouble. The former frowned, then started to open his mouth. It was then that Fargo drove the Henry's stock into Lafferty's side with such force that Lafferty was jolted backward, crashing into the counter and half sprawling across it. Rufus, belatedly, snorted like an irate bull buffalo and clawed for his Remington, but he was pathetically slow, molasses in motion. Fargo swept the Henry's barrel up and around, clipping Rufus across the temple. The tall gunman crumpled like a sheet of paper and lay on his side, a scarlet rivulet seeping from a nasty gash.

Corncob Bob was agape in astonishment. His thick lips worked like those of a carp out of water, and it was a full ten seconds before he collected his wits and blurted, "What do you think you're doing, mister? I don't allow no rough stuff in my place."

Fargo leveled the Henry, the muzzle inches from the trader's huge belly. "You didn't object to these two polecats roughing up the girl."

"Why should I? She's a mangy squaw." Corncob Bob's forehead glistened with beads of sweat. "What are you, anyway? Some kind of Injun lover, or something?" His forefinger speared at the woman. "I'll have you know she's mine to do with as I darn well please. Just a couple of weeks ago I gave her pa a heap of trinkets so she could come and live with me for a year."

Fargo's dislike of the man increased by leaps and bounds. The poor maiden was quaking like an aspen leaf in a gale, and he read in her gaze the gratitude she did not utter aloud. "What I am is starved."

Corncob Bob glanced at the Henry. His Adam's apple bobbed and he mustered a wan smile. "Sure, mister, sure. I don't want no trouble. I'll have the boys wait until after you're done." To the girl he hissed, "Get cracking, instead of standing there like a bump on a log. Be sure and fix everything proper, too, or there will be hell to pay."

The maiden nodded and went to leave.

"Hold on," Fargo said. "You never told me your real name."

"Winnemucca."

She was gone in a flash, with a swirl of her hair and a hint of a friendly smile, as graceful as an antelope, as beautiful as a spring day. Fargo felt a familiar hunger that had nothing to do with food, and a stirring in his loins.

"Stupid Injun names," Corncob Bob said. "Who can pronounce those tongue twisters? I call her Sue, after a cow my pa had on our farm back in Ohio when I was a boy. Come to think of it, Injuns are about as dumb as cows, ain't they?"

Fargo nearly lost his self-control. He came so close to slamming the Henry into the trader's vile mouth that he had to back away. Rufus was out cold, but Lafferty had shaken off the effects of the blow to his rib cage and was uncurling, hatred contorting his rodent features. The small gunman's hands hovered over the Smith & Wesson.

"Nobody does that to me and gets away with it. Put down that rifle, hombre, and let's see how tough you really are."

Rather than indulge the killer, Fargo pointed the Henry at Lafferty's chest. "You've got it backwards. Shuck the gunbelt and let it drop. After I leave you can pick it up again. But if you so much as touch it before then—" Fargo thumbed back the hammer to emphasize his point.

Lafferty was livid, a living powder keg primed to explode. His fingers clenched and unclenched and he grit his teeth in a feral snarl. "I don't take my guns off for anyone."

"Suit yourself," Fargo said and fired into the front of the counter a hand's width to the gunman's left. Corncob Bob squealed and jumped, but Lafferty did not so much as bat an eye. "The next one will go right through you." Again Fargo curled back the hammer, and when it clicked, the hardcase promptly shed his hardware, letting them *thunk* onto the floor.

"You'll pay, you son of a bitch. Mark my words."

Fargo did not doubt for a moment he had made a bitter enemy and that Lafferty would try to make worm food of him at the earliest opportunity. A smart man would shoot the gunman dead on the spot. Or so Fargo sought to convince himself. But he had never gunned down an unarmed person in his life, and he was not about to start. Having scruples had its drawbacks, he reflected. "Any time you feel man enough."

Lafferty glared as Fargo returned to his chair. If looks could kill, the gunman would have shriveled Fargo like a withered plant.

Rufus stirred to life and sluggishly sat up. "What in tarnation happened?" he mumbled, blankly blinking. Then he stiffened and gingerly touched the gash. "Now I remember." Heaving to his feet, he swung toward the tables. "You hit me, you varmint."

Fargo already had the Henry pointed in the right direction. Elevating it a hair, he casually asked, "Ever seen what a .44-caliber slug can do to a man's insides?"

Rufus had not seemed to realize the rifle was trained on him until that moment. Taking a step backward, he hiked up both arms and bleated, "Now hold on there, stranger. Maybe I was a mite hasty. Let's forget the whole thing, shall we?"

The plea was as counterfeit as fool's gold. The tall hard-case was not the sort to forgive and forget, and they both knew it. Fargo had been in similar situations too many times to be fooled. The two buzzards would bide their time and bushwhack him when it suited them. "Do like your friend did and shed the six-shooter."

It was remarkable how swiftly a man could unbuckle a belt when properly motivated. Rufus slowly lowered it, careful not to scrape the Remington. As he straightened, he remarked, "I never did catch your handle, mister."

"I never mentioned it." Fargo laid the rifle down and pretended to ignore the pair as they huddled and whispered, no doubt making plans to execute their revenge. Both cast repeated smoldering glances his way. Corncob Bob, chewing on the stem of his pipe, came over bearing the whiskey bottle and set it on the edge of the table.

"Here you go, friend. Wait until you taste this tornado juice. It goes down as smooth as can be."

The trader's spittle was dribbling over the label. Fargo did not even bother to pick it up. "Fetch a new bottle."

"Huh? What's wrong with this one?"

"Nothing a ton of lye soap couldn't cure." Fargo leaned back and waited while the heavyset proprietor complied. His thoughts drifted to Camp Douglas, an army post situated on a bench overlooking Salt Lake City. The federal government had established it to protect the Overland mail and telegraph and keep tabs on hostiles, or so the politicians claimed. But they weren't fooling a soul. The real reason the post had been set up was so the government could keep a tight rein on the Mormons.

A week ago Fargo had stopped there on his trek east and had encountered an old acquaintance, Colonel Tom O'Neil. That evening as they sat reminiscing about their Arizona days O'Neil had abruptly changed the subject. "Ever hear of the Chemehuevi tribe?"

Fargo had. Whites called them the Southern Paiutes, or Digger Indians, a derogatory nickname. It stemmed from the practice of the Chemehuevi men of carrying pointed sticks used to pry wild vegetables and roots from the soil. Foragers, they roamed the land in small bands, barely eking out a living. They were a poor tribe—the poorest of the poor. Fargo had never had any personal dealings with the Chemehuevi, although he had run into their kin, the Northern Paiutes, on occasion. "What about them?"

O'Neil had fidgeted, acting uncomfortable about bringing up the subject. "I know about the time you spent among the Sioux when you were young. It explains why you've always been friendly to the Indians, why you're not one of those who believes that the only good redskin is a dead redskin." Pausing, he had toyed with a button on his uniform. "I really have no business imposing on you, but word has leaked back to me that the Chemehuevi are having a hard time of it."

When Fargo offered no comment, the officer continued. "I'd look into the rumors myself, but I have my hands full with the Mormons. There is talk of another rebellion, in case you haven't heard. And all because our government won't let them practice polygamy any longer." Catching himself, O'Neil said, "But back to the Chemehuevis. Their problem doesn't really fall under military jurisdiction. Nor will the civil authorities look into it unless they receive complaints and—"

"What exactly is the problem?" Fargo had interrupted.

O'Neil leaned forward. "Vague reports have filtered to me through some of my scouts. Reports of Chemehuevis being beaten and whipped, and of a chief who was hung. I know it's none of your affair, but I was hoping you could look into the situation and get word to me if it's as bad as it seems."

So here Fargo was, seated in a trading post in the heart of Chemehuevi territory, a trading post that had no business being there. Not if Corncob Bob counted on making a living at it. No trappers roamed the nearby mountains, no settlers or ranchers lived in the vicinity. In short, there was no one with whom Bob could trade other than the poverty-stricken Chemehuevis. Fargo's reverie ended as the trader deposited a new bottle at his elbow. "Much obliged."

The whiskey was everything the man had claimed. It burned a path clear down to Fargo's stomach, warming him through and through. Shortly thereafter the food arrived. Winnemucca brought it on a large tray, deftly balanced on her head. The eggs and steak had been done to perfection, and Fargo savored his first bite of each.

"Is it all right?" Winnemucca asked hopefully, anxious to please. Up close he could not avoid noticing how her bosom swelled against her dress, and the shapely outline of her hips and thighs. It was enough to set his loins to twitching again.

"Better than that. This is downright delicious." Fargo motioned at the chair across from his. "Have a seat. I'd like some company."

Winnemucca stole a glance at the counter. Corncob Bob had overheard and gave a vigorous shake of his moon head. "I can not, sir, as much as I would like to. I may only talk to customers when they have paid for the privilege. It is one of Mr. Newton's many rules."

"Rules be hanged." Fargo nudged the chair with the tip of a boot. "Sit a spell. I'm after some information and you might be able to help." He took another swallow. "Have you by any chance heard of a Chemehuevi chief being hung by white men?" That was all O'Neil had been able to tell him. No name, no location, no other details.

A hush descended. Lafferty and Rufus stopped whispering and glanced around so sharply they were in danger of throwing their necks out. Corncob Bob Newton froze in the act of reaching for a glass. Winnemucca recoiled as if she had been slapped and lost all the color in her sun-bronzed cheeks. Much too quickly she said, "No, I have not. Now if you will excuse me."

Fargo was out of his chair before she had gone two steps. Lightly gripping her arm, he said, "Hold on. I need to get at the truth. I won't let any harm come to you, if that's what you're afraid of."

Winnemucca placed a warm hand on his. "Please. Whoever you are. You have been kind to me, so I will give you advice you must take. Finish your meal and go before you get into a lot of trouble."

"Too late for that, squaw," said Corncob Bob.

Skye Fargo shifted to tell the trader to mind his own business. The words died on the tip of his tongue at the sight of a double-barreled shotgun fixed on his midsection. At that range the scattergun would blow him in half.

2

The Trailsman had no one to blame but himself. He had been inexcusably careless. He had taken it for granted the two gunmen were the only serious threat and as a result he had not kept an eye on Newton. Now he imitated a statue as Corncob Bob smirked and hefted the shotgun, a fat thumb resting on one of the twin hammers.

"You had your nerve, mister, lecturing me a while ago about keeping my nose out of other people's business," the trader said resentfully. "Especially when you go sticking yours into everyone else's."

Winnemucca started to move between them but Corncob Bob growled for her to stay put. "Please," she said. "He has done no harm. Let him go."

"No harm?" Newton said, bobbing his chin at the gunmen. "Rufus and Lafferty would disagree." Raising the scattergun to his shoulder, he sighted down the double barrels. "Tell me, friend. What are you doing here? You wouldn't be a federal marshal, by any chance?"

"I'm no lawman," Fargo said.

"Where did you hear about an Injun being the guest of honor at a necktie social?" the trader demanded. "I didn't think it was common knowledge other than hereabouts."

"Then it's true." Fargo saw the hardcases reclaiming their gunbelts. He gauged the odds of diving out the entrance before a load of buckshot cut him in two and decided not to make the attempt. Shrugging, he said, "It was just a story I heard, is all."

"Who told you?" Corncob Bob probed.

"I can't remember."

"Well, you better recollect who it was, and right quick, or me and the boys are going to show you what we think of snoopy busybodies who think they have the God-given right to ride roughshod over everyone else." Bob sidled to his left to come around the end of the counter. Not once did the shotgun dip or sway.

Lafferty strutted forward, strapping his matched set of Smith & Wessons around his lean waist. "Well, well, well. I reckon the boot is on the other foot, ain't it?" he said, gloating. Shoving Winnemucca, he stopped in front of the Trailsman and made a show of balling his fists and rapping his knuckles together. "All of a sudden you don't seem so tough to me, big man. Why do you think that is?"

Rufus tittered as he stalked up from the rear. "We're going to have us some fun. Yessirree." He brushed a forefinger across the gash on his temple. "I owe you, mister. Let's see if you can take it as well as you dish it out."

Fargo suppressed an impulse to grin. The pair had blundered, and for all their bluster they weren't savvy enough to recognize their mistake. So long as he had been standing there by himself, Corncob Bob could turn him into a human sieve if he so much as twitched a finger. But now both gunmen were in the line of fire. Newton dared not shoot or he would hit them, too.

"Take this jasper's hog leg, Rufus," Lafferty directed. "Then we can learn him some manners."

Fargo tensed as the tall hardcase reached for his Colt. He waited until the very last instant, until Rufus's fingers were about to close around the butt. Then he exploded, whipping an elbow back into Rufus even as he drove his right foot up into Lafferty's groin. So quickly did he strike that both gunmen were caught off guard. Corncob Bob yelled, "Get out of the way!" and tried to get a clear shot but Lafferty staggered between them.

Rotating on the ball of a foot, Fargo delivered an uppercut to Rufus as Rufus spread both arms to pounce. The blow rocked Rufus on his heels but he did not go down. A glance showed Newton circling to the right. Immediately,

Fargo closed on Rufus, deliberately grappling with the dazed gunman to prevent the trader from firing.

"Let me at him!" Lafferty raged. For a small man he was a scrapper, and he tore into Fargo with his fists flying.

The punches were wild, inflicting no serious injury. Fargo absorbed them without flinching while pivoting so Lafferty and Rufus were in Corncob Bob's sights, and not him. Rufus had recovered and lashed out in fury, his fists rock hard. Unlike Lafferty, he had a smidgen of boxing experience and threw his punches where they would do the most damage. One caught Fargo on the side of the neck and briefly rendered half of his face numb. Another landed just below a kidney, lancing Fargo with excruciating agony.

"Out of the damn way!" Corncob Bob fumed at his friends. "I can't unload my cannon with you two jackasses there."

In the flurry of excitement, Winnemucca had been all but forgotten. Fargo glimpsed her darting to his table and snatching the whiskey bottle. A bound put her behind the trader. Newton was venting his spleen of lurid swear words when the heavy bottle crashed onto his skull, shattering the glass. Newton tottered, almost regained his balance, then folded at the knees and melted to the plank floorboards, the scattergun thudding beside him.

Now Fargo was free to deal with the gunmen unhindered. Ducking under a swing by Rufus, he rammed his right fist into Lafferty's abdomen. The ratty gunman was smashed backward and tripped over Corncob Bob. Rufus roared like a grizzly and clamped a hand on Fargo's throat. Fargo batted at the tall hardcase's wrist but it was like hitting an iron bar. He brought his right leg up to deflect a knee to his privates, then, twisting, he levered Rufus into the counter with a resounding crash.

Momentarily in the clear, Fargo took a short step to the right and kicked Lafferty on the chin. The hothead was rising, stabbing a hand at one of his revolvers. Catapulted into a table, Lafferty brought it down on top of him when he slid unconscious onto his side a few feet from Newton.

Only Rufus had any fight left. Pushing onto his knees, he

suddenly flung himself at Fargo's shins and wrapped both arms around Fargo's legs. "Damn you to hell!" he yelled. "I'm going to pound you to a pulp!"

Fargo felt his feet being hauled out from under him. Entwining his hands, he hammered them on Rufus's head but it was like hammering an anvil. As he landed on his back, he coiled his legs. Rufus had let them go and was about to leap on top of his chest. But the soles of his boots slammed into the tall gunman first, driving Rufus back against the counter with a loud *crack*. Rufus cried out and arched his spine.

Flashing upright, Fargo executed a combination that stretched Rufus out, senseless and bleeding from the lower lip. Breathing hard from the exertion, Fargo stepped to the counter and leaned on it to catch his breath. He had been extremely lucky. Had either of the gunmen thought to resort to their hardware while he was busy with the other, he'd be pushing up grass come next spring. "Thanks for the help," he said to Winnemucca.

The Chemehuevi maiden was aghast. Hands pressed to her cheeks, she whispered more to herself than to him, "What have we done? They will punish us as they have punished others! My father and mother will be whipped, or worse. I must beg for forgiveness."

"Who will punish you?" Fargo asked. She was so distraught that he walked over and draped an arm around her shoulder. "Don't fret. I promised to protect you, remember? If these are the three who hung your chief, I'll see to it that they go up before a judge."

"No, no. You don't understand." Winnemucca's wide eyes roved the room and settled on the shotgun. "We must kill them, now, before they wake up, before they can tell the others." She bent to pick up the scattergun but Fargo would not let her.

"What others? What exactly is going on here?"

"Please," Winnemucca insisted, wriggling from under his arm. "You do not know what you are up against. There are too many for you to fight alone. They will hunt us down and hurt those I love if we do not slay these three."

Fargo could not bring himself to murder anyone in cold blood, even vermin like the three who littered the floor. "Why don't we sit down? You can tell me what has been going on around here, and how these three fit into the scheme of things."

A sound outside gave Winnemucca a start. Grasping his sleeve, she said, "If you refuse to do as I say, you leave us no choice but to flee before any of the others show up. We must warn my parents. Afterward, we will hide until it is safe to move about again, until Pike's man have stopped hunting us."

Twice that name had been mentioned. "Who is this Pike?" Fargo inquired. "A friend of Newton's and Lafferty's?"

"He is evil, a wicked person who has brought ruin to my people." She clutched at his buckskin shirt. "I beg you. We must leave before his men come. Four or five of them stop by every day about this time."

The urgency in her tone spurred Fargo to action. "All right. Grab your things and we'll head for the stable." Dashing to the Henry, he spun to race out but stopped on finding she had not moved. "What's wrong?"

Winnemucca plucked at her dress. "This is all I brought with me." Scowling at the prone form of Corncob Bob, she said, "I want nothing else. Certainly nothing of his."

Clasping her hand, Fargo hurried outdoors. The harsh glare of bright sunlight made him squint. He was almost to the edge of the porch when a threatening snarl alerted him to the trio of four-legged brutes who ringed it. Fang, Slash, and Ripper were crouched low to the ground, their lips curled back, their powerful bodies rigid. Fargo tucked the Henry to his side. "Stay behind me. If they rush us, run back inside."

"No," Winnemucca said. "You can not stop all of them before they reach you. Let me try to calm them. They are used to me." Bravely venturing onto the steps, she held out her hand and said, "Come, Fang, come."

The mongrel growled and slunk forward. Afraid it would tear into her, Fargo fixed a bead on the dog's forehead. The maiden smiled, holding her ground, her poise remarkable. Fang crept steadily closer as Slash and Ripper converged from either side.

"Smell me," Winnemucca coaxed. "You know my scent. And you know that you are not to harm me." Aside, to Fargo, she said softly, "The first day I was here Fang tried to bite me and Newton beat him so badly I thought he would die."

The big dog was near enough to lick her hand. Sniffing loudly, Fang slowly rose to his full height and fell silent. Following his cue, Slash and Ripper likewise relaxed. Winnemucca patted Fang's head and scratched behind his ears, earning a couple of licks. "See? We are old friends, you and I."

Fargo lowered the Henry. Descending the steps, he angled toward the stable. To the northwest a tiny dust cloud spiked his interest. Riders, evidently, on their way to the trading post. "Would they be Pike's men?"

Winnemucca looked and gnawed on her lower lip a moment. "I can not say for sure. Usually they come in from the south. But if it is them, we are as good as dead once they learn what we have done."

"Then let's light a shuck before they spot us."

The Ovaro had eaten over half the hay and was reluctant to stop but Fargo guided the stallion from the stall, threw on his saddle blanket, then the saddle itself. He assumed that Winnemucca would help herself to one of the other horses but he was wrong. When he finished cinching up, he was annoyed to find her standing beside the door, patiently waiting. "What the hell?" he declared. "Pick out a mount."

"But they are not mine. It would be stealing. I thought I would ride double with you."

Exasperated, Fargo hastened to the next stall. In it was a mare, Lafferty's mare, apparently, since it was the only one there. He did not bother with a saddle. Most Indian children, boys and girls alike, were taught to ride bareback soon after they learned to walk. Sliding a bridle on, he practically flung the reins at Winnemucca. "Here. And don't give me any guff." She hesitated, then accepted and swung agilely astride the animal's back. Fargo forked leather and trotted from the building, noting as he reined to the south that the dust cloud had increased in size. Another five minutes and the newcomers would arrive. "You lead the way."

Winnemucca urged the mare past the pinto and turned to the southwest. Fang, Slash, and Ripper were by the porch and did not try to stop them. Once in the open, she held to a gallop. Her dress hitched up around her knees, every now and then showing a tantalizing hint of her silken thighs. Fargo could not help but imagine what it would be like to caress those flawless limbs and to feel her cherry lips on his.

Soon the heavy hooves of their horses had raised another dust cloud, yet it could not be helped. Fargo checked over a shoulder again and again without detecting any trace of pursuit. Perhaps Lady Luck was with them and they would get clean away, or so he hoped. In the distance reared jagged buttes mingled with outlandish rock formations. Arid country, where game was scarce and water scarcer. Where only the hardiest animals and men survived.

For over an hour they traveled, until Fargo was completely convinced no one was after them. By then the Ovaro and the mare were lathered with sweat. In the shade of a stone monolith over fifty feet high they finally drew rein and dismounted. Winnemucca was a bundle of nerves and commenced pacing back and forth.

Fargo's stomach grumbled to remind him he had never finished his meal. Rummaging in his saddlebags, he located a small bundle of pemmican given to him by friendly Shoshones. "Care for some?" he asked as he unwrapped the folded piece of hide and selected a morsel for himself.

"Thank you, no. I am too worried about my mother and father." Winnemucca was a study in anxiety, her habit of chewing on her lip in times of stress in no fashion detracting from her appealing allure. "Pike will have them killed. We must reach them before he does."

Biting into the pemmican, Fargo hunkered and remarked,

28

"You still haven't told me who he is and why you're so all-fired scared of him."

"You would be, too, if you knew what he has done." Winnemucca shuddered as if cold, then came over to squat beside him. "Pike Cutler is his name. He came to our country over two winters ago with a dozen men as cruel as he is. When he showed up at our village, my people made them welcome, as we have always done with white men. We shared what little corn and nuts we had to spare. We were as nice as could be." Her voice broke. She had to cough and swallow before she could go on. "And how were we repaid? With violence and bloodshed."

Fargo did not comment when she paused. Narrating the ordeal was upsetting her greatly but it was important he learn all the details if he was to help the Chemehuevis.

"At the time we were camped on the banks of the stream that your people know as Ash Creek. Pike Cutler smoked the pipe of peace with our chief, Wavako, then asked to be taken to a certain valley in the heart of our land. Red Valley, the whites call it. Cutler said he had heard about the valley from an old trapper who visited us many winters ago with the man our people named the Beaver Hunter."

That would be Jedediah Smith, Fargo guessed, one of the most famous of all the trappers, a fearless adventurer whose feats were legendary. Smith had been the first American to reach California overland from the Mississippi, the first to cross the imposing Sierra Nevadas, the first to reach Oregon by going up the California coast. In one year alone he collected six hundred and twenty-eight beaver pelts, an incredible feat when you considered that the average trapper was fortunate to bring in three hundred.

Like Meriwether Lewis, the renowned explorer, Jed Smith met his end at an early age. In his case bandits were not to blame, but Comanches. Smith had been guiding a large party through drought-stricken land toward Santa Fe. They had been three days without water and Smith had gone on ahead to find some. As fate would have it, he did, but in hiding around the water hole had been a Comanche hunting party. Smith managed to kill their leader before a dozen lances and knives put an end to his career.

Fargo knew the story well, as he did those of all the mountain men and trappers who had blazed trails before him. They were his mentors, in a sense, for by learning all he could about them, in particular the mistakes they had made, he increased the likelihood of his living to a ripe old age.

Winnemucca had resumed her tale. "We had no idea why Pike Cutler wanted to see Red Valley. But Wavako took him there, as he requested, even though it has always been special to us. And when we got there, Cutler and his men claimed it for their own and have been there ever since. They make us work for them, and have their way with the women of my tribe."

"You're telling me that Cutler and the others are *living* there?" Fargo said. It made no sense, no sense whatsoever, for a bunch of white men to set down roots in country so dry and barren that even most Indians shunned it. Not when so much fertile land was available elsewhere for anyone to stake a claim on.

The maiden nodded. "Four moons ago Bob Newton came. Cutler's men helped him build the trading post and some of them went with him to Salt Lake City for the supplies he needed."

The mystery deepened. What link was there between Pike Cutler and Newton? Why had they gone to all the trouble to establish a post where no one in their right mind ever would? And what did Cutler hope to gain by his insane shenanigans? Fargo had to admit he was intensely curious to find out. "Your people must hate Cutler," he said.

"With a hatred as deep as the great canyon far to the south," Winnemucca said bitterly. "We would kill him if we could. But we are not fierce fighters like the Apaches or the Comanches. Our weapons are no match for the guns of his men." She shook with the intensity of her pent-up anger. "We have always tried to live in peace with others, and look what it has brought us."

Fargo did not reply. Along with the Shoshones and the

Flatheads, the Southern Paiutes were ranked as one of the friendliest tribes anywhere. Those other tribes, though, could defend themselves when attacked and boasted many fine warriors. It was a sad but true fact that even other Indians looked down their noses at the Diggers. The Utes and others never bothered to raid them because the Diggers owned nothing worth stealing. And no warrior worthy of the name wanted to count coup on an enemy so pathetically puny.

"Wavako thought we could live in peace with this Pike Cutler," Winnemucca was saying. "But he was wrong. He was shocked when Cutler showed his true nature and turned on us. But at least he was brave enough to speak out. Wavako told Cutler that we would not stand still for being treated as animals." A flush of emotion choked her into momentary silence. "For that, they hung him."

Fargo stopped eating. "You saw it happen?"

"No. None of us did. Cutler's men came for him in the middle of the night. They beat Wavako's woman when she tried to stop them, and dragged Wavako from his lodge. The next morning he was found hanging from a tree, his tongue sticking from his mouth, his face all purple and black." She closed her eyes and groaned. "We wanted to cut him down and bury him. But Cutler would not let us."

"He left the body swinging in the breeze to rot?"

"No. He set Wavako on fire. And he made us watch."

Fargo had encountered some nasty characters in his wide-flung travels, men who would slay their own kin for a handful of coins. Coldhearted murderers, wanton butchers who killed for the sheer thrill of killing, callous monsters who could snuff out the lives of innocents as casually as the average person swatted a fly, he had met them all, but he had never run into anyone despicable enough to burn a corpse out of vicious spite.

There was no doubt about it. The Chemehuevis needed help. But as Colonel O'Neil had pointed out, their plight did not fall under the army's jurisdiction. The ugly truth was that the military had more interest in exterminating the Indians than in safeguarding them.

Contacting a federal marshal would not do much good, either. Most lawmen would rank Wavako's death low on their long list of priorities. Despite flowery talk by politicians to the contrary, white justice was mainly for whites. The only time most lawmen took note of Indians was when Indians harmed whites. Whites harming Indians was another story. Lawmen rarely bothered to do anything about it.

The thought made Fargo simmer with indignation. The Indians deserved better treatment. He would be the first to admit there were bad ones, just as there were bad whites. But most were decent, kind people. Many, like the Chemehuevis, simply wanted to be left in peace to live as they saw fit on land that had been theirs to roam since the dawn of time. Unfortunately, as more and more whites eagerly flocked west of the Mississippi, the Indians were being pushed off their land or confined to small parts of it. As a result conflicts were more frequent. If the current state of affairs persisted, Fargo was of the opinion that eventually the tribes would rise up in unprecedented numbers. The plains and the mountains would run red with blood.

"Wavako's death crushed our spirit," Winnemucca said. "My people hang their heads in misery and shame. Cutler has set himself up as our lord and master, and we are powerless to resist."

"You say Cutler has a dozen gunmen with him?"

"At first there were twelve. Now there are well over twenty. A few more come every month. He has boasted that one day he will have his own army."

The more Fargo learned, the more mystified he grew. What did Pike Cutler want with that many curly wolves at his beck and call? Was there a lot more to all this than met the eye? The only one who could answer those questions was Cutler himself, and somehow Fargo doubted he could just walk up to the man and ask him, "Where are all your people now? At Red Valley?"

"No. The young women are there, and many of the young men. They are the ones who must work the fields." Winnemucca clenched her fists so hard that her nails bit into her skin; Fargo saw blood trickling down her palm. "At night the women must do other things, awful things. The rest, the old ones and the children, are camped along a stream a day's ride from the valley. That is where I am taking you."

"Does Cutler bother the old ones?"

"Only if they talk against him. Or if a son or daughter makes trouble." The maiden looked at the ground. A friend of mine and the man she loves, Konako, tried to escape from Red Valley. Cutler's men caught them and brought them back. They thought they would be killed. But Cutler sent for their mothers and fathers. To teach all of us a lesson, as he put it, he had the fathers whipped. The mothers were roped and dragged by Cutler's riders until they were torn and bleeding. No one has tried to escape since."

Fargo had learned enough. "Take me to your folks. We'll hold a council and work out a plan."

Winnemucca glanced up. "A plan to do what?"

Before Fargo could respond the stillness of the wastelands was broken by a faint, fluttering howl that rose eerily to a throaty peak, then died. Standing, Fargo faced the way they had come. "The damn dogs."

"Corncob Bob has put Fang, Slash, and Ripper on our trail. That is how Cutler caught Konako and Mika. Newton liked to brag to me that his hounds can track anyone, anywhere. Before he came here he used them to hunt raccoons and white men who escaped from prison in a place called Georgia."

"I wish you told me this sooner," Fargo remarked. He would have made more of an effort to hide their tracks and disguise their scent. "Mount up." There wasn't a moment to lose. That howl meant the three mongrels were hot on their trail.

A series of baying cries shattered the air as Winnemucca led Fargo around the imposing monolith and broke into a gallop. Fargo guessed that the mongrels were no more than half a mile behind, if that. While the horses were faster, the dogs had more stamina. Experienced man-hunters and coon killers would know to pace themselves. In an endurance test in that grueling heat the mongrels would outlast the stallion and the mare.

On across the blistered landscape Fargo and the maiden fled, the dust they raised a beacon that would make it easier for their four-legged pursuers. Sure enough, before too long a chorus of deep-throated howls warned that the hounds were no longer relying on scent alone. Fargo shifted in the saddle and swore.

In the distance were three dark specks that rapidly grew larger. In long, loping strides the man-hunters streaked across the ground, running shoulder to shoulder in a tight pack, closing in for the kill.

3

Skye Fargo pulled alongside Winnemucca and matched the stallion's gait to the mare's. The Ovaro could go faster but he would never desert the maiden, even if the dogs were snapping at their heels. Which soon became a distinct possibility. The mongrels had exceptional speed. Within five minutes the baying brutes were less than a hundred yards off.

Shucking the Henry from the boot, Fargo twisted, tucked the stock hard against his shoulder to compensate for the movement of the pinto, and fixed a bead on Fang. Or he tried to. Firing while at a gallop took great skill and no small amount of luck. He levered a round into the chamber, steadied the barrel as best he was able, and carefully banged off a shot. The slug kicked up dust in front of the dogs, missing Fang by a good half a yard. Instantly, the mongrels veered to the left and then commenced to zigzag so they would be harder to hit. Newton had taught them well.

Fargo searched for a spot to make a stand, somewhere he could protect Winnemucca and the horses, a spot where the dogs could not get at them except head-on. Rocky spires and ridges stretched to the far horizon. To the west reared a high mesa. None offered a haven. Suddenly a dry wash appeared directly in their path. "Rein up!" Fargo hollered as he thundered to the bottom and brought the stallion to a sliding halt. Vaulting from the saddle, he dashed up the slope and sank to one knee. Sixty yards out were the dogs, their broad muscular bodies low to the ground, streamlined living engines of destruction that could rip a man to shreds.

Fargo sighted on the one on the right and quickly fired. Again he missed, though not by much.

As if on cue, Fang, Slash, and Ripper spread out. Incredibly, they also increased their speed. Now they were molten flashes of sinew and claw, hurtling toward the wash like bristly cannonballs. They bayed as they charged, a nerve-rending chorus that would terrify most prey and freeze their quarry in helpless fright.

Not Skye Fargo. He managed to get off another shot and this time he had the satisfaction of seeing Slash go down. But the dog did not appear mortally stricken. In the blink of an eye it was back up and rushing toward him, wicked teeth bared, savagery incarnate. Fargo settled the Henry's sights smack between its eyes but his finger had just touched the trigger when a bestial snarl warned him one of the others was much closer. He whirled just as Fang leaped, the heavy dog smashing into his chest and bowling him over. Down he tumbled in a spray of dirt and dust. He heard Winnemucca cry out as he heaved to his knees.

Fang and Ripper both were there, both on him in a twinkling. Glistening teeth seemed to be everywhere, snapping, biting, slashing. Fargo slammed the stock into Ripper, pivoted, and clubbed Fang over the head with the barrel. All it did was anger them further. Ripper growled and darted in close, his teeth shearing into Fargo's thigh. Fargo lifted the rifle to bring the stock crashing down, and as he straightened, Fang barreled into him again, knocking him flat on his back.

Fargo stared death in the face. A hairy, twisted, fang-filled visage materialized above him and Fang's teeth arced at his throat. He had lost his hold on the Henry so his only recourse was to throw his left arm up. Agony speared through him as Fang's teeth crunched in a feral vise. He felt blood, felt a numbing sensation. In desperation he grabbed for his Colt and cleared leather. To his right Ripper appeared, mouth wide, going for his neck. Fargo put two slugs into the dog at a range of six inches. Ripper stopped abruptly as if he had crashed into a brick wall, then folded to the earth.

Meanwhile, Fang was trying to bite clean through Fargo's wrist. Fargo lunged upward but the mongrel was too heavy. Claws ripped his shirt, his legs. Suddenly he caught sight of Winnemucca above Fang's shoulders. She held a big rock in both hands and brought it down with all her might on top of Fang's head. Without a sound Fang keeled over and lay oozing blood from above an ear.

Fargo shoved into a crouch. Of Slash there was no sign. He scrambled to the top of the wash, his hurt arm tucked to his side, the Colt cocked and extended, and was bewildered to not see any trace of the third dog. "Where in the hell did it get to?" he exclaimed.

Winnemucca sprang to his side. She had retrieved the Henry and knelt. "You wounded him. Maybe he went off to die."

Fargo was skeptical. Yes, many animals crawled off to be alone when their time came, but Slash had rebounded right away after being shot. He doubted the mongrel was dead, or even seriously hurt.

"You're bleeding badly," Winnemucca said, reaching for his left arm.

"It will have to wait. We're getting out of here while we can." Fargo was worried that Newton and the gunnies were close enough to have heard the shot and would come on at a gallop. Steeling his mind against the terrible pain, he half slid down the slope and ran to the stallion. In order to mount he had to hook his right arm around the saddle horn and pull himself up. Inadvertently, he smeared blood on the saddle. The lower half of his sleeve was soaked and so was his shirt where he had pressed his wrist against it. Unless he tended the wound soon, he stood a very real chance of bleeding to death. "Let's go."

"What about your gun?" Winnemucca asked, waving the Henry.

"Hold on to it for a while."

At the top they paused long enough to scour the terrain they had covered. As Fargo dreaded, tendrils of dust over a mile to the northeast pinpointed where the trading post owner and his cohorts were. "Ride like the wind," he directed, and did so himself, his left arm against his stomach. A wave of dizziness afflicted him but he shrugged it off and kept on riding. They had to put as many miles as they could behind them before nightfall.

"Are you all right?" Winnemucca called out.

"Fine," Fargo lied. He was as weak as a newborn kitten and his thinking was befuddled. Worse, the whole left side of his body tingled as if it were falling asleep. The pain in his arm was enough to make him gnash his teeth. Sweat trickled over his brows and into his eyes, stinging them unbearably.

For another hour the Trailsman pushed the horses to their limit, and beyond. The sun was a red jewel blazing on the brink of the world when he finally slowed to a walk. He was tingling all over now and he had to hold on to the saddle to keep from falling. Every so often tiny bright dots swam before his eyes. His throat felt as if someone had poured sand down it, while his left arm was aflame. Both eyes were bleary, his vision so blurred that he could not see objects clearly at more than thirty feet.

A hand fell on his good arm. "Look at you. You are in no shape to go any further. We will stop soon, whether you want to or not."

Fargo did not argue. His head was pounding mercilessly, and it was all he could do to stay on the pinto as the maiden guided him toward a hill. Exhaustion caused him to slump forward and close his eyes. He only intended to rest a few moments to gain his strength. So he was dumbfounded when he opened them and found himself on the ground with a blanket covering him to the chin. Nearby a small fire crackled. On a makeshift spit pieces of rabbit were being roasted. Winnemucca was nowhere to be seen. Alarmed, he sat up and promptly regretted being impetuous. His temples hammered and the night sky spun and danced. He felt sick to his stomach and had to lie back down.

"Don't strain yourself, Skye."

An angel with raven hair and a ravishing smile hovered over him, holding his coffeepot. "Rest until supper is ready.

I found a spring up the ravine and have watered the horses."

Fargo had to swallow several times and moisten his mouth before his thick tongue would move. "Thanks. I'd like to help out, but—"

Bending, Winnemucca lightly pressed a finger to his lips. "Hush. No apology is needed. You have done more than most men would do, all for someone you hardly know." Her finger drifted to his cheek and caressed him. "You are a remarkable man, Skye Fargo."

"I'm a thirsty man," Fargo amended. As she turned to the fire, he saw that the hem of her dress was uneven, as if she had cut strips from it. He could guess why. Weakly lifting the edge of the blanket, he confirmed that his left wrist had been competently bandaged. "I'm in your debt," he croaked.

"Nonsense. You saved me at the trading post. Now we are even, as you whites like to say."

The aroma of the roasting meat sparked a rumble from Fargo's stomach. He closed his eyes again, relieved that for the moment they were safe. When he opened them, he was puzzled to note the stars had changed position and a quarter-moon had risen. Another hour or more had gone by.

"Are you ready to eat?"

Winnemucca was silhouetted by the fire, her jutting bosom in sharp profile. She was sipping from his tin cup, her long legs curled under her, her luscious thighs accented by the swell of her dress.

"I'm hungry enough to eat you," Fargo quipped and was rewarded with a scarlet tinge in her cheeks. She brought a stick on which several pieces of rabbit had been neatly skewered. When he reached for it, she playfully swatted his hand.

"Just rest. I will feed you."

No healthy, red-blooded man would ever refuse such an offer. Fargo was content to lie there and bite off mouthfuls when she lowered the stick to his lips. Once her fingers brushed his mouth and lingered. She stared intently at him the whole time, her eyes smoldering pools. Reading her thoughts was child's play. At length she coughed to clear her throat and asked huskily, "Do you have a wife?"

"No. And I'm not in the market for one, either."

Winnemucca took the hint. "Nor am I looking for a husband. I only asked because many white men pretend they do not have wives when they do. They lie to get what they want, and when they have gotten it, they go back to their wives and lie about where they have been and what they have done. I am glad you are not one of those."

"I've never had to deceive a woman to get her interested," Fargo said. It was not a boast, simply a statement of fact.

"No, a handsome man like you would not have to. There is something about you. Something that stirs a woman deep inside. Something that makes her hungry, but not for food." To demonstrate her point, Winnemucca leaned down and delicately touched her soft, warm lips to his. She tasted sweet as sugar. Fargo parted his mouth and slid his tongue out. She responded by sucking on it as if it were a straw, igniting sparks in his loins. Raising his good arm, he fondled her shoulder, then slipped his hand lower to cup her breast. It swelled under his palm, the nipple as hard as a nail, eliciting a groan from Winnemucca.

Fargo tried to shift so he could reach lower but the dizziness returned. He struggled to keep from passing out, his body going momentarily slack. The maiden straightened and regarded him with concern.

"You risk too much too soon. It is better if you finish your meal and sleep."

The last thing Fargo wanted was to rest. His manhood had stirred to full attention and he yearned to pull her down beside him. But his traitor body had notions of its own. Mentally fuming at the dogs and the fickle whim of happenstance that conspired to render him helpless, he lapsed into sullen silence. It did not take much meat to fill his belly. He washed it down with a cup of coffee, then curled onto his right side.

"Rest easy, handsome one. I will stand guard," Winnemucca said as she tucked the blanket around his neck.

Fargo felt guilty leaving the chore to her. By rights he should help out, but in his condition he would be worthless. He'd doze off, more than likely, leaving them vulnerable to an ambush. "It's just not right," he muttered. Another second, and he was out to the world, adrift in a maze of dreams punctuated by a bizarre nightmare in which hundreds of dogs were after him. Not normal dogs, but outlandish creatures, some with spikes and horns and bony crests, some with six legs or eight, some with two tails or two heads, others with forked tails and no ears. Dogs unlike any ever known. Dogs spawned in the innermost recesses of his darkest imaginings. He eluded them for the longest time, running across a freakish blue plain covered by red grass and yellow trees. At length he came to the edge of a cliff so high that a river at the bottom was a tiny orange ribbon. He whirled to run off but it was too late. The pack had him at its mercy. Growling and roaring and foaming at the mouth, the horrible dogs converged. He shouted at them and swung his arms to drive them back but they paid no heed. Before long the biggest of the pack coiled to leap. Madly he darted to the right and the left. They had him hemmed in. Suddenly the big beast leaped. He locked his fingers in its throat to hold it at bay but its momentum carried them both over the rim. Down they fell, falling forever it seemed, the ground hurtling up to meet them. Just as he was about to be dashed to his doom on jagged blue boulders, he woke up.

Fargo blinked and gulped, still seeing the dogs in his mind's eye. Perspiration caked him and he was breathing heavily. Stars still ruled the heavens. The fire had burned out, embers smoldering among charred limbs. Winnemucca sat propped on his rifle, sound asleep. He opted not to wake her. In another hour or two it would be dawn. If the cutthroats had not attacked yet, they were not likely to until after sunrise.

The coffeepot was on a flat rock well beyond his reach. Thirsty enough to drink one of the Great Lakes dry, Fargo stiffly sat up and pushed off the blanket. The rest had done him a world of good. His head no longer spun and he had a wealth of energy. His left arm, though, was so sore he could barely move it. The bandage had stopped the bleeding but his wrist was swollen to twice its usual size and the slightest movement was torture.

Fargo rose anyway, slowly, testing his legs before he put his full weight on them. The coffee was cold so he fanned the coals, added busted limbs from a pile the maiden had gathered the night before, and soon had a fire going. Sliding the flat rock closer to the flames, he set the pot on it and sat back.

Some of the meat was left, stuck on a stick imbedded in the ground. Fargo treated himself to a piece and nibbled while he waited. It helped restore enough of his strength that he felt able to lead the horses up the ravine to the spring. The chill morning air was invigorating. In the distance a coyote yipped and was answered by another. Somewhere an owl uttered the eternal query of owls everywhere. In the brush a small animal skittered about, another rabbit, he suspected.

Fargo had a lot to think about. He was due on the Bear River in another couple of weeks, but that could wait. The Chemehuevis needed him. Hell, they needed *anyone* willing to stand up to Pike Cutler. And he was just the hombre to do it.

Fargo never had been able to stand back and do nothing when those who could not defend themselves were put in peril by heartless sons of bitches like Cutler. Women in distress, pilgrims in need, or, as in this instance, Indians being mistreated, all stirred an instinctive urge deep inside of him. He liked to tell himself it was perfectly natural. He liked to believe most men would do the same. But that really wasn't the case. Many would turn their backs on the Chemehuevis without a qualm.

A woman he met once on the Platte River claimed to know why he went around helping those who could not help themselves. She had compared him to those knights in shining armor that once roamed Europe and England, and claimed he was a knight in buckskins. He had laughed at her nonsense, of course. The knights of old had not indulged in whiskey and cards every chance they got. And many had taken vows of chastity, which he would never do in a million years. But maybe, just maybe, that woman had been closer to the truth than he was willing to admit. Why else was he about to buck twenty-to-one odds to aid a tribe he had never met?

Fargo led the horses back down the narrow game trail. Already a pink tinge framed the eastern horizon. Winnemucca was up and looking all around. On spotting him, she hurried into the ravine and shook a finger in reproach.

"What do you think you are doing? You are in no shape to go walking off by yourself. What if you start bleeding again?"

Walking down to her, Fargo dropped the reins, gripped her rounded bottom with both hands, and mashed her against his groin. His lips found hers and locked. She stiffened in surprise, then melted, her left hand entwined in his hair, her legs rubbing his. Her intoxicating earthy scent filled his nostrils, and he keenly desired to throw her down and take her then and there. But he had to keep Newton and the gunmen in mind. When he broke the kiss, Winnemucca inhaled loudly and gazed at him in wonderment.

"What was that for?"

"Another taste of things to come," Fargo promised. Her upturned face was unspeakably gorgeous, her lush figure as ripe as ripe fruit. A lump formed in his throat and he had to turn away before he lost control. "As for my wrist, it's fine. We'll head out at first light."

It was amazing how delicious cold rabbit and hot coffee could taste. Fargo wolfed his food and drank four heaping cups. As the golden crown of the sun heralded the new day, he emptied the dregs from the pot and cleaned it while the maiden saddled the stallion. She was not accustomed to using one so it took longer than it should have.

Presently they were under way. Fargo felt like a proverbial new man. If not for his wrist, he would be fit enough to wrestle a grizzly. He rode with the Henry resting crosswise against the saddle horn in case he needed to bring it into swift play. Winnemucca was on his left, and every so often he would catch her giving him peculiar searching looks. What it portended he had no idea.

Most of the morning had gone by when they crested a rise and before them unfolded a narrow plain through which a small gurgling stream meandered. At the far end of the plain a pair of hills flanked the stream, and it was here the Chemehuevis were encamped. Winnemucca pulled ahead, straightening and waving when a group of men tilling rude patches of pumpkins and corn spotted them. Shouts brought other members of the tribe on the run.

Fargo had heard all about how poor the tribe was. He should not have been shocked by what he found but the accounts did not do their plight justice. As Winnemucca had mentioned, mostly older Chemehuevis and children were present. The men were nearly naked, the oldest among them so scrawny it was a marvel they could get around. Some of the women wore rundown buckskin dresses. Others wore skirts but no tops and displayed no false modesty over exposing their pendulous breasts. Few of the children wore any clothes whatsoever, and like young ones everywhere they scampered playfully and created quite a racket.

The tribe's poverty was also reflected in their dwellings. Crude, insubstantial affairs made from long limbs of cottonwood and willow mixed with dried corn stalks, the lodges appeared flimsy enough to be blown away by the first strong wind.

Only a few horses were in evidence and they were as scrawny as the oldsters. No dogs were to be found, probably, Fargo mused, because any dogs the tribe obtained wound up in cooking pots.

Fargo became the center of suspicious stares as the Chemehuevis ringed the Ovaro and the mare. Only when Winnemucca addressed them in her own tongue did they adopt friendly smiles and several of the men came forward to shake hands as was the white custom. Fargo was introduced to Mevviwan, the elder who had assumed the mantle of tribal leader after the brutal slaying of Wavako. A kindly eyed, thin man who always spoke in a whisper, Mevviwan agreed to hold a special council that afternoon.

Winnemucca had been scanning the scores of faces since they arrived. As she finished translating, a smile lit her own and she ran to an elderly couple who embraced her with great affection. Cinonak and Koomah, her mother and father, greeted Fargo warmly, and invited him to their lodge. It was situated in the shade of the right-hand hill. Fargo had to stoop to enter. The floor was dirt, the interior gloomy. Personal belongings lined the base of the flimsy circular wall. Cinonak started a small fire in the center, under a convenient ventilation hole in the conical roof.

Winnemucca and her parents talked at length, and it was obvious that Winnemucca was intensely upset. At last she turned to Fargo and said in resignation, "They will not listen. I have tried to explain that Newton will come here after me. I have told them that if he does not find me, he will hurt them as he has threatened to do many times if I ever ran away. I have begged them to go off and hide, but they refuse."

"Tell them they can go with us," Fargo suggested. "We'll protect them."

"I already have." Winnemucca sadly regarded her parents. "They say that they are not afraid. They do not need protecting. This is their home. These are their people. So here they will stay."

"Will your father fight if Newton tries to harm them?"

Moisture glistened in her eyes. "My father has never lifted a finger against anyone. He believes all people should live in peace as brothers."

"Even after what happened to Wavako?" Fargo asked in amazement. He'd met devout Quakers and others who practiced brotherly love, sincere sorts who always turned the other cheek. And he respected their convictions. But if he had adopted the same outlook, long since he would have been planted six feet under. Most frontiersmen were more partial to the attitude a savvy parson had once expressed during a street-corner sermon. "Love your enemies, my brethren, but keep your guns well oiled." Then with a wink the minister had added, "And it might be best, in this land of heathens and hellions, to love your enemies from a distance. Remember what the Lord Himself said, 'Do not give what is holy to the dogs, nor cast your pearls before swine.'"

Fargo's personal philosophy was even more simple. If others treated him kindly, he treated them the same. If they tried to ride roughshod over him, then he'd do unto them as they did unto him. With a vengeance.

Now Fargo studied the serene visage of the Chemehuevi elder and knew he would be wasting his breath if he tried to persuade the couple to leave. But he had to at least try. "Ask your father outright if he wants to die."

Winnemucca translated. "He says that he loves life too much to want to cast it off. But he has no fear of the other side. If it is meant to be, it is meant to be, and nothing he or anyone else does can prevent it."

Fargo glanced at Cinonak. She was one of those people who always wore a cheery smile. She had an air of inner contentment about her that complemented her husband's serenity. "Doesn't Koomah care if Cinonak is murdered?"

Again Winnemucca relayed the question, her frown deepening at the answers she received from both her folks. "My father says of course he cares. He loves her as much as he loves life. But it would be wrong for him to go against what they both believe." She paused and tenderly put a hand on Cinonak's shoulder. "My mother does not want him to fight back, either. All she asks is that they die together so they can be together in the next world as they have been here."

Overcome with emotion, Winnemucca bowed her head and did not speak for the longest time. Cinonak busied herself preparing a meal of pinon nuts, sunflower seeds, chopped onions, and corn. Koomah happily pulled out a chipped-stone knife and commenced sharpening it.

Fargo was at a loss. Short of trussing them up and throwing them over a horse, he didn't see how he could get the couple out of the village before Newton's bunch arrived. He was also beginning to better appreciate the larger problem he faced, namely, how to stir up the Chemehuevis so they would rise up against Pike Cutler. If they all shared

Koomah's sentiments it would be impossible. They had rightfully been branded as human sheep, and the wonder of it all was that a mad wolf like Cutler had not come along long ago to slaughter or enslave them. He hoped the young men of the tribe were not as meek. Which reminded him. "I didn't see any younger men when we arrived. Didn't you tell me there were a few Cutler had not taken to Red Valley?"

Winnemucca dabbed at her eyes with a sleeve. "There are—" she said and got no further. Into the lodge rushed a boy of ten or twelve who bubbled excitedly while gesturing to the northeast. Winnemucca clasped her hands to her chest and stared wildly around like a doe caught in a trap.

"What is it?" Fargo asked. As if he could not guess.

"White men are coming. Eight of them, with many guns. And two dogs."

4

The eight stick figures were only half a mile away but none of the Chemehuevis showed any panic. They went on about their daily business as if nothing out of the ordinary were taking place.

Fargo darted to the horses and grabbed the mare's rein to hand them to Winnemucca. She was by the entrance, beseeching her parents to leave. Fargo did not need a translator to tell him how they responded. Winnemucca grew frantic and pulled at Cinonak but her mother calmly pried her fingers loose and gently pushed her toward their mounts. Sobbing, Winnemucca seized Cinonak's wrist and refused to let go.

Koomah intervened. Smiling lovingly, he separated them, held his daughter firmly, and steered her to the mare while speaking softly into her ear. Tears cascaded down the maiden's cheeks in a torrent of anguish. She clutched her father and motioned for him to climb on but he hoisted her astride the horse instead. Swinging toward Fargo, Winnemucca practically wailed, "Please! Do something. We can't let them die."

The Trailsman took a step, intending to clip the old man on the jaw and take him along whether Koomah liked it or not. Suddenly, though, a dozen other elders were there, surrounding him, forming a living wall between him and the parents.

Fargo was forced against the saddle and left no recourse other than to climb on. As much as he wanted to help Winnemucca, he couldn't bring himself to lift a finger against the Chemehuevis. "You're making a mistake," he said, realizing they would not understand. Or did they? Koomah gazed up at him with a sorrowful expression, pointed at Winnemucca, and reached up to grasp Fargo's hand.

Just then one of the others smacked the pinto on the hindquarters. Another did the same to the mare. Fargo glanced back as he paralleled the stream and saw the Chemehuevis moving toward the middle of the village. Winnemucca was crying in earnest, her despair so overwhelming that Fargo had to snatch her reins and guide the mare himself. Circling the hill, Fargo trotted up the brush-choked slope until they were below the crest. Sliding off, he eased onto his hands and knees and crawled.

The gunmen were a couple of hundred yards out. Newton, Lafferty, and Rufus were there, as well as five men Fargo had never set eyes on. Two of the mongrels, Fang and Slash, loped in the lead, neither limping or otherwise any the worse for wear after the clash in the dry wash. Yet he was sure he had put a slug into the latter, and the conk on Fang's head had been hard enough to split the skull of most dogs.

The Chemehuevis awaited the whites without qualm. Mevviwan was in the forefront, arms folded, his craggy, weathered face inscrutable. He raised a hand in greeting as the white men reined up. Corncob Bob Newton unlimbered his scattergun and announced loudly enough for Fargo to overhear, "Let's make this easy on everyone, shall we, you stinking savages? I want Winnemucca. Hand her over and none of you will come to grief."

The Chemehuevis stood motionless, smiling or grinning, or with their hands outspread to demonstrate they were peaceful.

"Quit stalling," Newton snapped. "I know some of you can talk our lingo, so answer me or I'll cut loose on this old fart." He pointed the shotgun at Mevviwan. "What will it be? Will you use some sense for once?"

A lanky Chemehuevi at Mevviwan's elbow responded in halting, clipped English. "So sorry. Winnemucca not here."

"Like hell she ain't." Corncob Bob bristled. "We tracked her and that tall feller clear from my trading post. And I lost a damn fine hound along the way. So fetch her, pronto. Fetch them both before my temper wears thin and I do something you won't like." When the Chemehuevis stood like bronzed sculptures and did not reply or move, Newton nudged his mount forward until it brushed against Mevviwan. "Don't trifle with me, you rotten Injun. I want that squaw and I want her now."

Infuriated by their continued silence, Newton slid down. "Suit yourselves. We'll do this the hard way, then." Lafferty and the rest of the gunmen dismounted, their rifles at the ready. "Fang, Slash," Corncob Bob said, "find me the squaw." From a pocket he removed what appeared to be a small washcloth. "Here's her scent again. Get cracking."

The hounds sniffed the cloth and were off, their noses to the ground. From lodge to lodge they roved, sniffing at each entrance, crisscrossing the village until, inevitably, they came to the dwelling that belonged to Winnemucca's parents and both let out with piercing howls. Newton and three gun sharks jogged over and barreled inside, the emerge seconds later with the trader livid. "They were here and they've gone, haven't they?" he demanded of no one in particular. "They reckon that they can do what they did to me and get away with it. But they're wrong. Dead wrong."

All this time, the Chemehuevis stood meek as little lambs. They stood there and they smiled and they made no attempt to prevent what happened next. Bob Newton stormed up to Koomah and Cinonak, spitting out, "Remember me? I'm the one who paid you for your gal. Dragged her off kicking and screaming, I did. And I warned you that if she ever ran away, or if she ever tried to stick a blade into me while I was sleeping, I was going to pay you another visit. Remember?"

Koomah grinned.

"Think it's funny, do you? Think you got the better of me? Think your gal can wallop me on the noggin and traipse off with that nosy son of a bitch and I'll just swallow my pride and do nothing? Well, you're wrong."

Fargo sensed what was coming and brought up the

Henry but he did not have it level when the scattergun discharged, booming as loud as a cannon. Koomah was blown almost in half, the buckshot tearing his abdomen to ribbons. Some of the Chemehuevi women screamed and all of the Chemehuevis whirled to flee but the other gunmen, unnoticed, had formed a line on either side of Newton and now they unleashed a withering volley that felled Chemehuevis like brittle grass in a hailstorm. Incensed, Fargo sighted down the barrel at Lafferty.

Slender hands wrapped around the barrel, jerking it aside. Winnemucca was gushing tears like a fountain. Her father had just been brutally slain yet she tried to twist the rifle from Fargo and said, "No. Don't. There are too many. You would only get yourself killed."

"I'll take the risk," Fargo said, and sought to remove her fingers. Down in the valley the Chemehuevis were fleeing across the stream, a human stampede soon lost amid the mesquite and shrubs. In their wake they left seven prone forms, four writhing in agony in pools of spreading scarlet. Rufus placed the muzzle of his rifle to the temple of a groaning man and cored the Chemehuevi's brain.

"What are we waitin' for?" Lafferty hollered. "Let's chase the vermin down and wipe them out."

Fargo tugged on his Henry and would have freed it had Winnemucca not thrown herself on top of the barrel, effectively pinning it to the ground. "Don't you want those butchers to pay?" he rasped, unable to understand her attitude. One minute she had been begging him to save her folks, the next she was stopping him from taking vengeance on her father's murderer.

"You know Pike's orders," Corncob Bob told the rat-faced gunman. "These savages are his leverage. The young ones will do anything he wants so long as he can hold the threat of exterminating their kin over their heads."

"Just a few more," Lafferty said eagerly.

Corncob Bob gestured. "Go ahead, you yack. But don't blame me when Pike opens your gut with that Bowie of his and strangles you with your own innards. Me, I'm not about to buck him. Not for all the gold this side of China."

The mention of Cutler dampened Lafferty's raw blood-lust. He contented himself with going to the twitching body of a girl half Winnemucca's age and pumping four shots into it. Moments later the hardcases had stepped into their stirrups. Corncob Bob pulled out his pipe to light it. "Truth to tell," he remarked, "if it were up to me I'd burn this whole village down around their lousy ears."

"What about the squaw and the stranger?" asked Rufus. "Do we keep on after them?"

"No, we do not," Newton said. "I have a post to run, and Pike won't like it if I'm away too long." He gazed at the hills, at the uncharted wilderness beyond. "We've chased them far enough. Sooner or later the squaw will show her face again, and when she does, I'll whip her within an inch of her life. As for that uppity feller, if he has any brains he'll light a shuck for parts unknown."

Fargo watched them depart in a swirl of dust, yipping and screeching like a pack of demented wolves. Fang and Slash were once more in front. He sagged onto his shoulder, numbed by the atrocity. "You should have let me drop a few."

Winnemucca dripped misery from every pore. Sitting up, she stared forlornly at her father's body. "He died as he lived. I disagreed, but I could not let you throw away your life for his sake. He would not have wanted you to."

"What about the others? Did they deserve to be gunned down?" Peeved, Fargo rose and swung onto the pinto. The folly of attempting to incite the Chemehuevis to revolt weighed heavily on him. Any tribe that could stand idly by while nine of their own were shot to pieces was poor warrior material. The Chemehuevis would be better off stealing away in the dead of night like the scared mice they were.

"Skye, wait."

Fargo went up and over the crest. A couple of the bodies were moving, offering hope they would survive. None of the Chemehuevis who had fled had reappeared so it was up to him to do what he could. Reining up beside an elderly man whose gray hair was spattered with red drops, he rolled the Chemehuevi over. A neat pink hole pulsed blood in the center of the man's sternum. For a few moments their eyes met and the Chemehuevi smiled. "Fools. The whole lot of you." Fargo grumbled. Closing the dead man's eyelids, he rose and moved to a woman attempting to crawl into a dwelling. The lower portion of her face had been shot away, and the only sound she could make was a low whine deep in her throat.

Fargo gently placed her on her side. Gnarled fingers enclosed his and although she had no mouth to smile with, she smiled with her eyes. It was the damnedest thing, the way these people accepted dying without complaint and went so peacefully into the hereafter. He squeezed her hand but she was already gone, expiring as silently as a puff of wind. As he had done with the man, he closed her eyes, then wiped his hand across his pants to remove crimson streaks.

"She was my aunt. We spent many happy times together when I was smaller."

Fargo turned. Winnemucca had stopped weeping but her eyes were haunted by the tragedy.

"I knew all of these people well. Some were relatives. Others were friends. Their loss leaves an empty space inside of me."

Some of the Chemehuevis were venturing back across the stream. They did not act stunned or horrified. They did not scream or rant and rave. As always, they behaved calmly, going from corpse to corpse and examining each with casual aloofness. Unbridled anger coursed through Fargo. Didn't they have feelings like everyone else? he wondered. What did it take to get them mad, *really* mad, so mad they would take up arms against their oppressors?

"I'm going to make sure Newton has left and isn't circling around to take us by surprise," Fargo said. In reality, he had a hankering to get away from the Chemehuevis for a while. Vaulting onto the stallion, he galloped after the killers and followed their tracks for over two miles. By then it was obvious Newton was bound for the trading post. Wheeling the pinto, Fargo retraced his steps, but he took his sweet time and spent it sorting his thoughts and plotting how best to proceed.

On entering the village he was startled to find the bodies were gone. There was no trace of them. Even the pools of blood had been covered by fresh layers of dirt. As for the Chemehuevis, few were abroad. Those who were, were going about their everyday routine as if they did not have a care in the world.

Fargo made up his mind to leave Winnemucca there and go to the Red Valley alone. He needed directions on how to find it, so he trotted to her parents' lodge. As he alighted, she came out. She had changed her dress for one much finer, one with fancier beadwork and longer fringe. It clung to her like a second skin, highlighting her charms in all the right places. Ordinarily, Fargo would have been mesmerized. But at the moment he was sick and tired of the whole tribe and hardly gave her a second look. All he wanted was to be shed of them.

"I was afraid you would not come back."

More gruffly than he aimed to, Fargo said, "I'd never run off and desert you. Unlike some people I can think of, I'm not as cold as ice inside."

Winnemucca stopped and gnawed on her lower lip. "You are mad at us," her womanly intuition divined. "Why? What have we done?"

"If you need to ask, I could never explain it," Fargo said. Pricked by guilt for being so harsh, he nodded at the dwelling. "Is your mother inside?"

"She has gone to her sister's. For a week she will be in mourning for my father. Until then, the lodge is ours if we care to share it."

The invitation in her tone could not be plainer but Fargo did not take the bait. "Don't tell me your people know *how* to mourn?" he asked crisply. It was a blatant insult, an uncalled-for snub, and it caused Winnemucca to blink and tense up. Fargo was sorry he had said it the instant the words were out of his mouth.

"I wish you would tell me how we have offended you."

Fargo faced her to do just that but an elder picked that

moment to pop out of nowhere and address the maiden. Listening, she grew somber. At the conclusion she indicated the hill across the stream and informed him, "A council has been called. You are invited to speak before the whole tribe."

"Now? What about the dead?"

"Those who died will be taken tonight and buried far from the village in a secret place known only to my people. It has been our way since the world was born." Winnemucca moved past him, then paused. "Are you coming? You gave them the idea that what you have to say is very important and they are anxious to hear it."

Maybe there was hope for them yet, Fargo reflected as he fell into step behind her. He tried to prepare a speech in his head but the enticing sway of the maiden's hips distracted him. He recalled her statement about sharing the lodge and decided he would like nothing better.

The village was virtually empty. A gravel bar at a shallow point enabled them to ford the stream without getting wet. Beyond, a trail wound to the side of the hill where over four dozen Chemehuevis were gathered in rows, the men higher up, the women lower down. Winnemucca escorted Fargo to a point above the men. "I will translate as you speak. The same with any questions they have."

Fargo looked down on the ranks of expectant faces and hesitated. He had never been one for flowery speeches. He always said what he had to say in as few words as possible. A friend of his liked to joke that he was as long-winded as a rock, and the friend had a point. As a politician he would be a flop because he always let his actions speak louder than anything he said. To stall he cleared his throat a few times.

"Don't be nervous," Winnemucca coaxed. "You are among friends."

"Then tell them this," Fargo began. "As a friend, I must warn them the bloodshed they saw today was only the beginning. If they think that by going along with whatever Cutler demands they will be spared from harm, they are dead wrong. I have met men like Cutler before, men who kill for the sake of killing. Men who would make wolf meat of every last Chemehuevi and never bat an eye."

Fargo could not tell if he was getting through but pressed on, warming to his topic as he went. "Anything worth keeping is worth fighting for. If the Chemehuevis want to keep their land, if they want to go on living as their fathers and their fathers' fathers before them have done, they must be willing to fight for the right to do so. Yes, I know Cutler's butchers have guns and the Chemehuevis don't. And I know all of you are worried about will happen to the young men and women in Red Valley if you make trouble." Pausing, Fargo raked every last one of them with a flinty gaze. "But I tell you now, with a straight tongue. Unless you rise up against Pike Cutler, there will come a day when the Chemehuevi dead will litter the ground like dead weeds and the way of life your people have had for so long will end."

He had not strung so many words together at one time in a coon's age. Fargo stopped to gauge their reaction. He had tried to get across what needed saying in terms the Chemehuevis would understand. But had it worked? A man in the front row had something to say, which Winnemucca relayed.

"If our enemies were Utes or Blackfeet we would fight for what is ours. But this man Cutler and those with him are whites. And we have heard what happens when our kind raises a hand against your kind. Many whites in blue coats will come, bringing many guns, and they will punish us. They will drive us from our land and force us to live where we do not want to live. So no matter what we do, we suffer."

Murmuring spread among them. The elder had raised a valid point. Fargo realized there was more to their reluctance to resist Cutler than their peaceable natures. Could it be he had misjudged them? "The army will not bother you if you fight back. You have my word on it."

"How can you be sure?" asked the same man.

Fargo picked his next words carefully, sensing that their final decision would hinge on his reply. "The army only cares when decent, law-abiding whites are attacked. If you were to raid a wagon train or a ranch or any of the small settlers around the great salt lake, troops would be sent to bring you before the white man's justice. But this is different. Pike Cutler and Corncob Bob Newton and the rest are a bunch of killers. The army would take *them* into custody if it had jurisdiction."

Another elder spoke. "What is this 'jurisdiction'?"

How could Fargo explain? Indians always had a hard time comprehending the white man's attitude toward things like owning land and administering the law. To them, it was as strange as Greek would be to him. "It means they are only allowed to act at certain times."

"Are we to understand that white justice is different for some whites than it is for other whites?" asked someone else.

"No, not exactly," Fargo was losing them. They were confused, uncertain, and less likely to go along with whatever plan he cooked up. "Think of it this way. If a Chemehuevi were to steal from another Chemehuevi—"

"That would never happen," declared the first elder.

"But if it *did,* say if a child stole something, who would punish him? The parents, or the rest of the tribe?" Fargo thought he was on the right track. Normally, parents punished their children. The parents had rightful "jurisdiction."

A man at the end of the second row stirred. "We do not punish our children," he said, with a hint of indignation that anyone dared suggest they did.

"Never?"

A woman answered. "We believe in always teaching our young ones to do right, not in hurting them if they do bad."

A different woman rose onto her knees. "We have heard that whites beat their children with belts and sticks. How horrible. We would never be so mean."

Fargo's patience was wearing thin. They had strayed completely off the mark. How could he make them see the light when the two cultures were so vastly different? "Forget all this business about punishment and answer a question. If the Utes were to attack the Apaches, would you attack the Utes to pay them back?"

"You are being silly," responded one of the taller men. "Why should we? Apaches are not Chemehuevis. It would not be any of our affair."

"And it's the same with the army. Outlaws like Pike Cutler are none of their affair. It's a job for a federal marshal, and right now the marshal has his hands full elsewhere." Fargo was bending the truth, but he did not know what else to do. Unless he incited them to take up arms against Cutler's gang, he would have to oppose the cutthroats alone.

Discussions broke out. Winnemucca looked at Fargo and said softly, "You have tried. For that, I thank you. But I do not think they will help. They are too set in their ways."

Fargo sighed and folded his arms. People were indeed creatures of habit. And, sad to say, some of those habits were impossible to break, even when breaking them was their only hope of salvation. "Can you think of anything to say? Something that will convince them I'm right?"

"Words will not convince them. They must convince themselves."

An elder in the uppermost row slowly stood. "We thank you, friend, for talking to us. We will consider what you have said. Each of us will voice what is in his heart. And when we are done, we will have an answer for you."

"How long will all that take?" Fargo inquired.

"Who can say? Two sleeps? Ten sleeps? A moon?" The elder bestowed one of those infuriating smiles on him. "Pike Cutler is not going anywhere. There is no need to hurry."

Like hell there wasn't, Fargo mused irritably. He was not going to twiddle his thumbs for a month while the Chemehuevis made up their minds. So be it, he thought. He had tried his best and it had not been good enough. From then on out, he would act on his own. "Palaver all you want to," he told them, and stalked down the slope in long strides that soon brought him to the bottom. The patter of footfalls preceded a hand falling on his shoulder.

"You are mad at us again? Why?" Winnemucca wanted to know.

Fargo turned. "I heard about a bird once. It lives in a place called Africa, and folks there call it an ostrich. The man who told me about it had been there on a ship, and he claimed that when ostriches were cornered by lions and such, they would stick their heads in the ground so they couldn't see what was about to eat them. I don't know if he was spinning a yarn or not. But your people are a lot like those ostriches."

"Because we have not fought back?" Winnemucca pursed her lips. "I think I begin to see your point. You would rather have us be like the Chiricahua Apaches, I suppose, and kill all outsiders who enter our territory? Or maybe we should be like the Blackfeet, who have always hated and butchered whites?"

"That's not what I meant at all," Fargo said, and left her. It was the final straw. When even the one person in the whole damn village who knew enough about whites' ways to get his meaning did not get it, it was time to light a shuck. He was so incensed he had half a mind to say to hell with the whole shebang and head for the Bear River. If the Chemehuevis didn't care what happened to them, why should he? Why knock himself out seeking to help people who could not be bothered to lift a finger in their own defense?

He waded across the stream instead of using the gravel bar, splashing water in all directions. Only the children and a handful of adults were in the village. A cluster of small ones took one look at his face and scattered as if he were a demon. An old crone retreated into her lodge. Evidently going around mad was something else the Chemehuevis did not abide. He saw the Ovaro grazing on dry grass beside Cinonak's lodge, and couldn't wait to fork leather. "Damn them all to hell," he berated the empty air.

Fargo was almost to the pinto when once more Winnemucca overtook him. Her warm hand brushed his neck. He pivoted so suddenly that she took a step backward in alarm. "What do you want now?" he demanded.

"I thought you might be hungry. I would like to invite you for food and drink and"— the maiden broke off, averted her eyes, and blushed—"and whatever else you would like to have."

There it was again. The veiled invitation. Fargo glanced at the pinto, then at her. At the swell of her twin peaks against the soft fawn dress, at her ruby lips and full cheeks, at the outline of her thighs and her small shapely feet. She was a beauty, a lush peach ripe for the picking. "I am a mite hungry," he admitted.

"I am glad."

Winnemucca bent to enter the dwelling. In doing so, her rounded buttocks were molded in contour by the soft buckskin. Skye Fargo licked his dry lips and followed her in.

5

In the suffused light of the interior Winnemucca's loveliness was magically enhanced. She stopped near the smoldering fire, and a sparkly sunbeam streaming in through the ventilation hole bathed her in its radiant glow, highlighting the flowery bloom of her smooth face and the fullness of her pert bosom. She gestured, a simple, graceful movement that in itself was powerfully alluring, and asked in a throaty purr, "What would you like?"

Fargo walked up to her and slid his arms around her waist. His mouth swooped to her cherry lips and he kissed her hard, mashing his lips while he pressed his chest flush with hers. The suddenness of his passion startled her, and she stiffened briefly, then draped her arms over his shoulders. Her mouth opened, admitting his tongue. He swirled it around her gums, her teeth.

Winnemucca moaned as their tongues entwined. Her breaths grew faster and hotter as his hands roved down her back to her posterior. His fingers groped her nether cheeks, kneading them, and he felt her legs quiver. When he broke for air, she tilted her head back, closed her eyes, and uttered a long, drawn-out sigh. "You make my heart flutter," she said.

Fargo intended to do a lot more than that. Lowering his mouth to her soft neck, he nibbled a path to her left ear and sucked on the lobe. In the meantime, his right hand strayed around the curve of her hourglass hip to her thigh, then drifted upward. At the first contact of his palm with her mount, Winnemucca gasped and dug her fingernails into his biceps. He could feel the heat from her simmering core through the dress.

It was a temptation to throw her roughly down, hike the dress to her waist, and plunge into her with sexual abandon. But no, he would rather take his time and savor the experience. Many a woman had told him that one of their biggest complaints about male lovemaking was the urge most men had to get it over with quickly. Women never could fathom why men had to act like elks in rut when there was more pleasure to be had when sensual hungers were sated slowly.

Fargo massaged the junction of her thighs until she was shaking like a leaf and her knees were on the verge of buckling. Carefully lowering her flat, he stretched out on his side and smothered her mouth with his. His hand found a breast, the nipple a spike that bit into his palm. He tweaked it through the buckskin and elicited a fluttering groan. She craved him as much as he craved her.

"Ohhhhh, I am so hot," Winnemucca said when Fargo dipped his lips to the nipple and gently drew it into his mouth.

That she was, an inferno to the touch, heated desire coursing through her veins. She lavished burning kisses on his forehead, his cheeks, his chin. She raked his broad shoulders and the muscles on his back so hard that she would have drawn blood if he were not wearing a shirt. Her knee slid between his legs and commenced to lightly pump up and down, sending exquisite sensations into his groin.

Fargo's pole was as rigid as a redwood. Sliding his left hand to the hem of her dress, he pulled it upward, revealing by gradual degrees Winnemucca's magnificent legs and silken inner thighs. He tugged it higher, above her slender waist, then halfway up her large breasts. She had to lift her back to accommodate him, and when she did, he hungrily clamped his mouth onto her right nipple.

Winnemucca arched her spine, her hips bucking against his. "I want you inside of me so much!"

Fargo aimed to oblige her but in his own good time. His hand covered her other glorious globe and kneaded it as if it were bread dough. She responded by hissing through her teeth and rimming her rosy lips with the tip of her own tongue. Her hand traced the outline of his chin, then rose to run through his hair, bumping his hat off in the process. After a while he licked a path to her navel and lathered it. Sliding lower, he kissed the marble flesh that bordered her full thatch. A tantalizing dank aroma enveloped him as she widened her legs to permit him easy access to the innermost sanctum of her womanhood.

Gliding his lips to her breasts, Fargo lowered his right hand to her Vesuvius. Her slit was soaked. It parted at the merest touch, allowing him to lightly stroke the tiny knob that was the key to unlocking a woman's deepest inhibitions. Her spine arched again and she cooed like a dove. When he rubbed the knob her eyelids fluttered and she sucked in air like a bellows. He knew just what to do to propel her to the brink of ecstasy. After a few minutes of his adept ministrations she was panting and squirming, a volcano fit to explode.

Fargo worked his hand lower. His forefinger rimmed her moist tunnel, causing her to cry out and clutch him as if she were afraid he would get up and leave. Holding his middle finger straight, he suddenly plunged it into her as far as the knuckle. She bit her lip to keep from screaming, then froze. In her eyes burned raw lust, lust she gave free reign when he began to stroke his finger in and out. It transformed her into a wanton firebrand. She dug her nails in deeper than ever, locked her mouth on his, and began to heave her backside skyward in rhythm with his strokes.

Her lips were honey, her tongue maple syrup made solid, her breasts cushions on which his chest rode as her hips pumped in steady cadence. It never failed to amaze Fargo how strong women were. Most gave the impression of being frail, an illusion fostered by their smaller bodies. But when a woman had to be, she was iron and grit and able to hold her own against most any man. Winnemucca was a case in point. Who would have suspected that someone so slender of stature could lift his entire body off the ground with deceptive ease?

Fargo unhitched his gunbelt and pants and they joined at the hips. The two were made one. His pulse and her pulse were matched to the beat of the same invisible drummer.

Lips glued, their legs thrusting in unison, they scaled the summit of their mountain of desire and were poised on the brink of the chasm of release. Fargo felt the mental dam he had erected to contain himself begin to crack. At the base of his skull a fiery ball of carnal excitement heated to a fever pitch.

"Ohhhhhhh! Skye!"

Winnemucca gushed, her legs wrapping around him tight, her arms enfolding him. They were in total elemental union, the fusion of their mouths and their sexual organs complete. Winnemucca was lost in rapture, and Fargo was about to join her. He held off as long as he could, held off until his throat was constricted and his lungs were near to bursting and his manhood was aching with the need to relieve the unbearable pressure.

"Please, Skye! Now!"

Fargo grit his teeth and struggled to prolong their pleasure but his organ had a will of its own. He spurted, sending a lightning bolt of pure delight shooting up his back and through his extremities to the tips of his fingers and his toes. It was nitroglycerin and thunder and a tornado all rolled into one. It was the single most fabulous experience known.

Fargo's senses swam. He lost all track of time, all track of anything and everything except the pure delirium of sexual gratification. On and on he thrust and thrust until his organ was spent. Gradually he coasted to a stop, dimly aware of the perspiration caking him, of Winnemucca's face nestled against his neck. For a short while all was right with the world. He was at peace with himself.

Sleep claimed him. Fargo awakened when a beam of sunlight fell on his face. Squinting up through the opening, he saw that the sun was on its westward arc. They had dozed for hours. He sat up and adjusted his pants. Rising, he strapped on the Colt, then reclaimed his hat. Winnemucca slumbered peacefully on, her breasts slowly rising and falling, her body resembling sculpted marble.

Against the wall was an old blanket. Fargo unfolded it and gently covered her in case someone should come to visit her while he was gone. Striding outside, he pulled his hat brim low and made for the stream. The village lay quiet under the hot sun. Few adults were abroad, and even most of the impish children were missing.

The water was deliciously cool. Fargo splashed some on his neck and down his shirt. Cupping a hand, he sipped to test the taste. Finding it agreeable, he knelt and drank enough to slake his thirst. As he straightened, a glimmer of light to the north caught his attention. It lasted barely a second, a brilliant flash that might have been caused by sunlight reflecting off a rock formation. Undoing his bandanna, he soaked it and wiped his face clean.

In another couple of hours the day would be done. Fargo was anxious to reach the Red Valley, and in that amount of time he could cover a lot of ground. He would have to wake up Winnemucca, though, for directions, and he was loath to disturb her. Bending his steps toward the village, he noticed several men talking in the shadow of a lodge. One was the lanky Chemehuevi who knew a smattering of English, the same one who had answered Newton earlier.

The men rose at his approach. "We help you?" asked the lanky one. He was middle-aged, his hair streaked with gray. The little finger on his left hand was missing.

"Where is Red Valley?" Fargo bluntly asked.

"Why? You go there?"

"Yes."

In his own tongue the Chemehuevi relayed the news to the others. Their smiles curled downward. "Maybe not good thing. Best you stay."

They were afraid he would stir up more trouble, Fargo reflected. But it was the only way to get to the bottom of the mystery, to learn what Pike Cutler was up to. "I'm going, with or without your help. So tell me how to find it."

The man hesitated. "Winnemucca know this? What she say?"

"She has no hold over me," Fargo hedged, then said, "I should think you would want my help. Once I know the whole situation, I'll go to the territorial governor and report what has happened. The government is bound to take action." He was not being totally honest. First, he had no intention of contacting the governor. Second, even if he did, the odds were slim that something would be done. The plain truth was that most state and territorial administrators cared as little for the Indians as the majority of the citizens who voted them into office. There had even been talk at the federal level of waging a campaign of outright extermination. Some years back, none other than President Andrew Jackson had advocated rounding up every tribe in the country as if they were cattle and herding them onto reservations. Those who resisted were to pay for their stubbornness with their lives.

The lanky man nervously fidgeted. "Maybe you right," he acknowledged at last. "I tell you." Pointing eastward, he said, "In one sleep you walk there. Not miss. Plenty big valley. Plenty big river."

Fargo thanked him. It was good news. On horseback he could be there in well under a day. Before noon tomorrow, he estimated. At the lodge he paused to peek in. Winnemucca was curled on her side, still sound asleep. Fargo regretted having to leave without letting her know, but she would try to talk him out of it or persuade her people to stop him. In order not to wake her when he rode off, he took the Ovaro's reins and walked the stallion to the stream. After letting it drink, he mounted and headed out.

On the far side of the plain were low hills. The land was arid, desolate, fit for lizards and snakes, not people. He pushed on until the sun had vanished and twilight was fading to night. In a gully he made a cold camp. Pemmican sufficed for his supper. For the stallion he gathered what scant grass he could find.

Years of sleeping under the stars had not dimmed his admiration for the heavenly spectacle. So many sparkled in the firmament that it was as if a gigantic swarm of fireflies hovered overhead. He fell asleep listening to a chorus of coyotes.

His internal clock woke him up right when he wanted. A faint pink band added a dash of color to the eastern sky as he threw on his saddle and swung up. Due east as the crow flies he rode, the landscape becoming drier, a parched hell that every living thing shunned. By the middle of the morning he was beginning to suspect the lanky Chemehuevi had lied. Then, abruptly, as he was on the verge of turning around, he struck paydirt.

Fargo was crossing another scorched plain. Waves of heat shimmered before him and he felt as if he were being baked alive in an oven, when without warning the earth yawned wide. He reined up, flabbergasted, and rose in the stirrups to gaze out over what had to be Red Valley. A better name for it would be Red Canyon.

Towering cliffs of red sandstone formed the east and west sides of a tremendous gash in the earth caused ages past by a geologic upheaval. A wide river flowed through the center and was bordered by tracts of woodland and green fields. It was a paradise in the midst of the wasteland, a Garden of Eden, so to speak, in the middle of Hell. So high were the cliffs that from Fargo's roost the people he could see moving about below appeared to be bugs. There were buildings and tilled acreage and a herd of horses in a wide pasture.

How to get down was the question. On a hunch, Fargo turned northward along the rim. Wisely, he stayed well away from the edge so he would not silhouette himself against the sky. About three-quarters of an hour later the ground began to slope gradually down toward the mouth of Red Valley. Verdant forest bordered the river at that point, so it was a simple matter for Fargo to gain the valley floor undetected. A wide trail bearing rutted wagon tracks led inward. Hooves had churned the dirt to dust, further proof the trail was regularly used, no doubt by Cutler's men when they traveled back and forth between Red Valley and the trading post.

Fargo rode cautiously, studying the tracks. He had gone no more than fifty yards when the metallic rasp of a rifle lever being worked snapped his head up. Quickly drawing rein, he stared at the two men who barred his path and mentally kicked himself for not being more alert.

"Lookee here, Rufus," Lafferty said cheerily. "Ain't this the feller who stomped us silly at Corncob Bob's?"

Rufus smirked wickedly, the rifle in his hands fixed on Fargo's chest. "Why, I do believe you're right, pard. What folks say must be true. It really is a small world."

Both the gunmen snickered at their little joke, then separated, Rufus bearing to the right, Lafferty to the left. The small hardcase flourished one of his Smith & Wessons, then touched a bruise on his ratlike face. "Every time I move my jaw I think of you, mister. And I dream of hearing you scream as we give you a taste of your own medicine."

Fargo said nothing, his hands out from his sides. Any sudden move would be his last.

"Look at him," Rufus said. "Plumb speechless, he is. Why, you'd think he was upset to see his old drinking pals again."

Lafferty shook his head. "It's not that. This big bastard is wonderin' how in the hell we got here, and why we were lyin' in wait for him. Am I right, mister?" When Fargo did not respond, he pointed the revolver. "I asked you a question, you son of a bitch."

What else could Fargo do? He nodded.

Beaming smugly, Lafferty stepped to the stallion and yanked the Henry from its scabbard. "It's like this, big man. Corncob Bob had a feelin' that you and that squaw were hidin' near the Digger village. So after we'd gone about five miles, he told Rufus and me to circle back and spy on them mangy Injuns." Leaning the rifle against his leg, he reached behind him and pulled a small folding telescope from his pocket. "This here spyglass comes in right handy sometimes."

Fargo remembered the flash of light he had seen while drinking at the stream.

"We saw you leave the village," Lafferty continued. "It wasn't hard to guess where you were going, so we hurried on ahead and have been waitin' for you to show." The pint-sized gunman cocked the Smith & Wesson. "I should thank you. I've always had a hankering to shoot someone's eyes out. And guess what? You're elected."

6

Skye Fargo had been caught flat-footed. He could make a stab for his Colt but he was only fooling himself. The outcome was inevitable. He might get one of them but the other would put hot lead into him. Still, he would not sit there and die meekly. It went against his grain. So long as life remained, so long as he drew breath, he would fight for his life to the best of his ability. But as he tensed to sweep his arm to his holster, he was given a reprieve.

"Hold on, pard," Rufus said. "Newton told us that Pike would likely want to talk to this hombre. We should tie him up and take him to the house."

"To hell with Corncob Bob," Lafferty spat. "He acts high and mighty just because Pike and him have been close friends for so long. I say we shoot this varmint here and now."

Rufus's thick brows knit. "I won't stand in your way. You know that. But if Pike asks, I'll have to tell him what you did, and I don't reckon he'll be very pleased. You know how he gets when he's riled. Remember poor Skinner? I never knew brains looked like that. Go ahead, though, if you have your mind made up."

Lafferty's smug air waned. "I ain't scared of Pike," he declared without much conviction. "But I reckon you have a point."

"Keep him covered, then," Rufus said, palming a Green River knife on his right hip. He cut a short length of rope from Fargo's own lariat and bound Fargo's wrists behind his back. Plucking the Colt free, he winked and quipped, "Just between you and me, stranger, you'd have been better off to go for your hog leg and let us shoot you. Pike Cutler is the meanest man on the face of the planet. He'll do things to you that would curl a Comanche's hair."

"Quit jawin' and fetch our horses," Lafferty complained.

The trail wound deeper into the thick forest, always adjacent to the river. Presently Fargo heard the ring of axes on wood. They came to a clearing in which a flatbed wagon was parked. On the box sat a stocky hardcase holding a shotgun. Another leaned against a rear wheel, a rifle in the crook of his arm. They were guards, watching over ten young Chemehuevi men engaged in chopping down trees and trimming the branches. The man on the seat looked up and called out, "Who you got there, Lafferty? A lawdog?"

"Don't know yet," the small killer said. "Whoever he is, he'll be buzzard bait before too long."

The Chemehuevis stopped work to stare. One, a strapping man of twenty or so, had corded sinews on his coppery arms and chest. When his dark eyes swiveled to Lafferty they smoldered with hatred.

"Get back to work, you lazy polecats!" bawled the guard on the wagon. "If you don't get done by sunset, you'll all be whipped tonight."

They complied, but the muscular man glanced at Fargo one last time. For a fleeting instant an unspoken bond was shared. Fargo nodded. The Paiute bobbed his chin. Then the trail reentered the trees and foliage obstructed Fargo's view.

In half a mile the woodland ended. Tilled fields replaced the trees, the crops being tended by young Chemehuevi women. They, too, were under guard. Only a few looked up as Fargo was led past by Rufus. He read fear in their eyes, fear and abject misery. Being enslaved did that. It broke the spirit, crushed the soul.

The horses in the pasture numbered over a hundred. Most bore brands, but as Fargo discovered, few of the brands were the same. The explanation was obvious and he could not resist commenting. "Seems like you boys have been busy helping yourselves to someone else's stock."

"What's it to you?" Lafferty snapped.

Rufus was more talkative. "Hell, mister, we're just getting started. Pike says that by this time next year we'll have us a thousand head, and we can sell them to the army for a mint. Between those critters and the gals and all the other stuff, each of us will be plumb rich before too long."

"The gals?" Fargo repeated quizzically.

Lafferty jabbed a finger at his partner. "Don't say another word, damn it. There's no need for this sidewinder to know what we've got goin' for us."

Beyond the pasture were the buildings. A large stable flanked a circular corral. A long, low structure, much like a typical bunkhouse, had been built between the corral and what could only be described as a mansion. Fargo guessed there must be fifty rooms, easy. Two stories high and constructed in a horseshoe shape, the mansion boasted sparkling white columns and a wide portico. It was the kind of house found on southern plantations, as out of place in Red Valley as formal evening wear would be on a Chemehuevi.

More young warriors were constructing another building under the watchful eyes of four tough characters. A dozen other leather slappers were present, some breaking in a bay at the corral, some lounging by the stable, others scattered around the trimmed front lawn. Fargo became the focus of attention as his captors guided the stallion to a hitching post close to the portico. A lean man who wore a black bowler hat and favored a nickel-plated pistol came around the corner of the mansion and hailed them.

"Lafferty! Rufe! What's going on? Who's that you've got there?"

"The nosy cuss who caused the ruckus at Corncob Bob's," Lafferty explained. "We caught the varmint sneakin' into the valley and figured Pike would want to have a heart to heart with him."

The man in the bowler studied Fargo. "My handle is Lucius Quay. Who might you be, friend? Something tells me I know you from somewhere."

Quay was right. Fargo recognized him as a gambler he had met in St. Louis a couple of years ago, a poor gambler, as Fargo recollected, and an even poorer loser. He kept silent.

"Cat got your tongue?" Quay asked. "Well, we'll loosen it before too long. One of our boys down by the corral has a knack for making folks talk. Hot irons, slivers under the nails, needles stuck in the ears, you name it, he just loves to hurt things."

Ten of the gunmen now ringed the stallion and there was not a friendly face among them. Lafferty and Rufus dismounted, Rufus hauling Fargo off the pinto and pushing him so that he stumbled against the post. Gruff mirth was suddenly stifled as every last man faced the porch.

A living mountain had stepped from the mansion. Fargo did not have to be told who it was; it could only be Pike Cutler. Close to seven feet tall, Cutler was as wide as a bull, as powerfully built as a grizzly. His legs were tree trunks, his chest a broad slab, his arms as thick as kegs of ale. He wore a suit and a plush jacket, superbly tailored. A craggy moon face split by a hawkish nose rested on a stub of a neck. Gray eyes that seemed to be flecked with specks of silver locked on the Trailsman and regarded him much as a panther might regard prey. "What's all the commotion out here, gentlemen?" he demanded in a voice reminiscent of gravel on tin.

Lafferty gestured. "This is the jasper from the tradin' post, Pike. Corncob Bob sent a rider to tell you all about him, remember?"

Cutler folded hands the size of hams behind his back and slowly walked down the steps. For such a huge man he was surprisingly light on his feet. "Are you implying, Mr. Lafferty, that my memory is so piss poor I can't recall an event that took place a day ago?"

"No, no. Never," the ratty gunman said quickly—a little too quickly.

"I sincerely hope not." Cutler's voice was an ominous thunderclap and lightning danced in his eerie eyes. Casually strolling to the hitching post, he leaned on it, his weight so massive that the pole sagged and threatened to break. "They tell me that you beat three men with your fists, stranger."

"I had some help," Fargo mentioned.

Cutler's moon face cracked in a grin. "Ah. Yes. The woman, Winnemucca. Truly a fierce fighter. No wonder Lafferty, Rufus, and Newton were soundly thrashed. If there had been someone else on your side, a ten-year-old, say, it is doubtful the three of them would still be breathing."

The insults caused Lafferty's mouth to crimp but he did not try to justify the outcome. Interesting, Fargo thought, all the more so because Pike Cutler apparently was not wearing a gun. Evidently Lafferty was so scared of Cutler that the gunman tolerated any abuse, even when Pike was unarmed. "The next time I'll try to see to it that they don't get up again," he said.

"The next time?" Cutler said, and chuckled. "I like a man with confidence, although yours is woefully misplaced. I have plans for you. Plans that will keep you in this valley permanently."

"As another one of your slaves?"

"Nothing so mundane, I'm afraid. You will provide our entertainment in two days. Saturday evenings we always do something special." Flexing his fingers, Cutler cracked his knuckles, the retort as loud as a small caliber gun. "You will provide us with fine diversion, I'll warrant."

The outlaw leader was not at all as Fargo had imagined. He'd pictured another grimy rodent like Lafferty, or maybe another ox like Rufus. Instead, here was a cultured man who would be at home in New York or any other big city, a man as out of place as the mansion itself. Fargo did not know what to make of it all.

As if Cutler had the ability to read minds, he said, "You must be wondering what is going on here." An expansive wave of his stout arm encompassed the entire valley. "Don't be upset if you are confused. Not many men are privileged to witness history in the making. This is a crucial cusp in time. You stand, sir, at the hub of what will one day be a sprawling empire. *My* empire."

"Planning to take over part of the United States for your own, are you?" Fargo jested.

"Yes."

Fargo waited for Cutler to smile or joke or otherwise show he was not serious. But, incredibly, the man was. "It must be the sun. Either it's fried my brain and I'm hearing things, or it's fried yours and you're loco."

Pike Cutler laughed, then straightened. "You have wit, sir. A rare trait among the primitives with whom I must deal daily."

Was he referring to the Chemehuevis or his own men? Fargo mused. "Mind filling me in on exactly how you aim to carve out your little kingdom?"

"Not at all. Why don't I do it over supper? Mr. Quay will bring you to the house at five-thirty."

Lafferty squealed like a rodent that had its tail stepped on. "You're invitin' him to a meal, boss? After what he did to Rufus and me? After all the trouble we had to go through to catch him for you? If you ask me, it would be smarter just to blow out his lamp and get on with what has to be done."

Pike Cutler turned astoundingly fast for one so ponderous. Moving to the small gunman's side, he rested a hand on Lafferty's slim shoulder. His thumb and forefinger squeezed ever so lightly and Lafferty winced in pain. "There you go again, insulting my intellect. If I didn't know better, I would swear you were trying to provoke me."

"Not me, boss," the hardcase blurted. "Sometimes I don't talk as good as I should, is all. The words comes out wrong."

Cutler did not remove his hand. Smirking at the ring of cutthroats, he said gleefully, "Who says a man needs more than a second-grade education?" With mercurial swiftness, his mood changed drastically. His features clouded and his voice grew as hollow as an empty tomb. "You test my patience, Samuel. You truly do. Why must I always explain my actions to your satisfaction?"

"I never—" Lafferty began, quieting when Cutler's thumb and finger pinched together again.

"Haven't you ever heard of granting the condemned a last hearty meal?" Pike said, with a wave at Fargo. "In two days this man will be dead. The least we can do is make them bearable. Don't you agree?" Not allowing the gunman to respond, Cutler went right on. "Besides, you know what I like to do on Saturday evenings. If we were to kill this man now, as you prefer, someone else must take his place. Are you perhaps volunteering?"

The change that had come over Cutler was minor compared to the one that now afflicted Sam Lafferty. Until that moment the gunman had put on a brazen front, but he could not quite hide the fear that lurked just below the surface. Now he gave up pretending. An ashen hue came over him. He swayed and gulped and broke out in beads of sweat. He was terrified, and he did not care who saw it. "No, sir," he said. "I don't want to wind up like Skinner. You can adopt this hombre for all I care."

"How compassionate you are," Cutler said with undisguised venom. "In the future, though, you would be well advised to control that wayward tongue of yours. Saying the wrong thing can get a person into all sorts of trouble." Suddenly wheeling, he commanded Lucius Quay, "Take him to the stable and keep him under guard until five-thirty. I expect him to be prompt."

"He'll be there on time."

"Excellent," Pike Cutler inhaled deeply. "Smell those flowers in the garden? Isn't the fragrance wonderful?"

No one spoke or moved until the front door closed behind him. A collective breath was released, and one of the hardcases near Fargo whispered to a companion, "I swear. Working for him is like working for a two-legged cottonmouth. You never know when he's going to strike."

"Hush, you idiot. If someone was to tell him what you just said, he'd use you this Saturday instead."

A pair of burly underlings gripped Fargo by either arm and ushered him toward the stable. Lucius Quay trailed along, deep in thought. Halfway there he said, "Come on, mister. Help me out. Your face is awful familiar. I'd bet my gold tooth we've met, but for the life of me I can't recollect where. Denver, maybe? New Orleans? Or St. Louis?"

Fargo's memory was better. They had played cards with three other men for over six hours, a grueling marathon of stud poker from midnight until dawn, until one by one the players were cleaned out, leaving only the two of them. The gambler's poke had been whittled down to seventy-five dollars. On their last hand, Quay bet it all on a pair. Fargo had been holding a full house. In spite Quay had flung the money across the table and stormed out of the smoky room.

Bales of hay were piled to the right of the stable door. Fargo was pushed onto one and told to sit. The burly two-some took up positions just outside but Quay came over and began to frisk him. "Almost forgot something." He paused. "Your handle is really bothering me. It's on the tip of my damn tongue but I can't peg you." He paused again. "Well, what have we here?" He had found the Arkansas toothpick Fargo kept in his right boot. "Reckon I'll keep this." Quay looked up. "Ever worked for the army? Scouting, maybe?"

Fargo had, but he did not admit it. Acting indifferent, he surveyed the stalls and loft. In a corner underneath was a pitchfork. The tack room was to the left, and propped against the wall beside it was a small scythe, the kind he had seen the women in the fields using. He quickly turned away so the gambler would not realize he had seen the implement.

Lucius Quay cocked his head. "This is aggravating, you know that? It'll come to me sooner or later so why not just fess up? I don't see what difference it can make. Pike isn't about to let you leave Red Valley alive whether we know who you are or not."

Fargo changed his mind about talking. The gambler's curiosity could be made to work in his favor provided he did not let any clues to his identity slip. Speaking in a higher tone than he normally would, he asked, "What's a card-sharp like you doing hooked up with a sorry outfit like this?"

Quay brightened, his smile displaying the gold tooth he had mentioned, prominent in the center of his upper set. "I knew you knew me!" He checked the doorway, then sidled a shade nearer. "I wouldn't underestimate Pike Cutler, friend. Sure, some of his gunnies leave a lot to be desired, but Cutler has enough brains for the whole bunch. Enough brawn, too."

"What's he up to?"

"Oh, no you don't." Quay chortled. "Don't even try to pry the information out of me. You'll have to wait until this evening. Cutler will tell you all you need to know, if it suits him."

Fargo uttered a mocking laugh. "I've heard enough already. Do you believe that nonsense about carving out an empire? If you do, you more loco than he is."

Lucius Quay was indignant. "Shows how much you know. What's to stop him? The whole southern third of the territory is unclaimed land, land nobody else wants except the few measly Indian tribes that live here."

Partial insight flooded through Fargo and he gazed out at the Chemehuevi men working on the new building. "Poor tribes," he said. "Tribes too weak to put up much of a fight if someone decided to take their land away from them. Someone like Pike Cutler."

"The timing couldn't be better." Quay gloated. "Here in Utah the army has its hands full with the Mormons. Out on the plains, it's the hostile Sioux and Cheyenne. In the East, there's talk of civil war. Now I ask you. With all that going on, what does the army care about a few stinking Indians?"

A chill ran down Fargo's backbone, as if an icy gust of wayward wind from a far-off peak in the Rockies had slipped under his shirt and across his skin. As madly insane as Cutler's wild scheme seemed, Fargo could not deny there was a method to the man's madness. Pike Cutler was vastly more cunning than Fargo had given him credit for. As impossible as it was to accept at first, the plan stood a very good chance of being carried out.

Cutler had chosen well. He had picked one of the most godforsaken spots in the entire country, if not the entire planet. A region no other white men had any interest in. There were no towns or farming communities. No homesteaders had moved into the areas. No ranches, either, because most of the region was too bone dry to support large herds of cattle. In short, there was no one to oppose him.

No one, that was, except a few puny tribes. Tribes like the Chemehuevis, the Kawaiisu, and the Washoe, tribes who owned few horses and fewer guns. Indians who made their living by foraging or tilling the soil. People who had always been friendly and peaceful. Trampling them into the dust—or enslaving them—would be child's play for any sizeable armed force, just such a small army as Cutler was in the process of forming.

Why hadn't Fargo seen it sooner? A determined man with limitless ambition could carve himself out a private empire that covered hundreds and hundreds of square miles. A domain larger than many states back east. And by the time the government got around to noticing, it would be too late. Especially for the Indians involved.

Only someone with an indomitable will could pull it off. Someone to whom human life meant as little as ants under his feet. Someone who was totally ruthless. A man who could kill women and children and still sleep well at night. A man who thought the sun rose and set just for his benefit. Someone exactly like Pike Cutler.

Lucius Quay was moving toward the door. "I've told you too much. I'd better quit jawing and get some work done. As Pike's right arm, I'm expected to stay on top of things for him. *Adios,* mister. We'll talk again later. Maybe by then I'll remember who in the hell you are."

The two guards were just outside, their backs to the stable. They were more interested in some Paiute women filing toward the mansion bearing baskets of fresh vegetables.

Fargo rose and crept toward the scythe. At any moment one of the gunmen might glance inside. He was glad straw littered the ground, cushioning his footsteps. As he got closer he saw that the handle was busted. The curved blade, though, was intact, and when he turned and squatted so he could grip it, he discovered the edge was sharp enough to cut his skin at the slightest pressure.

Rising, Fargo swiftly sidled toward the bales. One of the guards was rolling a cigarette while the other was ogling a petite Chemehuevi. Just as Fargo sat down, the second man looked into the stable. Satisfied Fargo was behaving himself, the man resumed watching the women.

So far, so good, Fargo told himself. Shifting his fingers so he gripped the scythe by the back of the blade, he aligned the keen edge so it rubbed against the first of three separate loops. Then he commenced sawing back and forth. It took some doing since he had to hold the scythe at an awkward, painful angle, but he persisted, stopping whenever one of the guards appeared to be about to turn.

As he sawed, he pondered. It was plain now that alone he had no hope of stopping Pike Cutler. Too many gunnies were at Cutler's beck and call. Since he could not count on the Chemehuevis for help, his best bet was to ride like the wind to Salt Lake City and report what was going on to Colonel O'Neil. If anyone could persuade the higher-ups to intervene, O'Neil could. He was a decent, honorable soldier.

The tip of the blade bit into his forearm. Fargo bent his wrists lower, tilted the scythe, and continued to cut away. He would have preferred to wait until after dark but he could not risk someone coming along and taking the scythe. He had a couple of hours yet before he was due to join Cutler at the mansion, which was ample enough time so long as he was left alone. He had to slice through each of the three loops without opening a vein.

Outside, the work slowed. Insects droned. The horses in the corral stood idle or nipped at grass. It was the hottest part of the afternoon, when men and animals alike grew sluggish. And inattentive, Fargo hoped. The guards had retreated into the shade to the right of the wide door, and he could only see one. The man paid no attention to him, which suited him just fine.

Two of the loops had parted and Fargo was working on the third when, without any warning, into the stable strolled

Sam Lafferty and a Paiute woman. She carried a tray bearing a pitcher and a glass. Lafferty was scowling and looked fit to tear into anyone who so much as gazed at him crosswise.

Fargo stopped sawing and sat perfectly still. The gunman had not seemed to notice his arms moving, but the woman had. Her dark eyes had narrowed and she was staring at his bent elbows. "What's this?" he asked casually.

"Something to drink," Lafferty said bitterly.

"How thoughtful," Fargo baited him. "And here I didn't think you had a kind bone in your body."

"I don't!" the gunman snarled. "If it were up to me, I'd let you rot." He motioned for the woman to set the silver tray down. "Pike Cutler made me bring it. Prattled on about good manners and the like." Lafferty swore luridly. "Damn foolishness, I say. When you're going to kill a man, kill him. Don't treat him like he's a guest at a fancy hotel."

"Cutler sure is a strange one," Fargo agreed. "Where is he from, anyway?"

Lafferty was not as gullible as Lucius Quay. "You can ask him yourself this evening when you're sittin' at his big mahogany table and eatin' off his china plates."

"I take it you don't like Cutler very much."

"Shows how much you know. I have nothin' against the man personal-like except that awful temper of his." Pivoting on the high heels of his boots, Lafferty took several steps to the right so he could see the mansion. "It's just that I don't understand him. Not one bit. I've seen Pike crush a man's skull with his bare hands and put a slug through a knothole at twenty yards. No one is tougher or a better shot."

"So what don't you understand?" Fargo prompted as he reapplied the edge of the scythe to the last loop. The woman saw his arms pump but she did not tell the gunman.

"How he can be so mean one minute and act like a dandy the next. Why, he reads poetry, for cryin' out loud. And with my own eyes I've seen him pick flowers and sniff 'em, just like a girl. He's different from most, Cutler is. If he wasn't so damned smart, I'd figure he was touched in the head."

The rope slid off. Blood trickled down Fargo's wrist but he didn't care. Reversing his grips so he held the broken handle, he glanced at the entrance. Neither of the guards were visible although he could hear them talking. Lafferty still had his back to the bales and did not see him slowly rise and pad forward.

"Oh, what the hell," the hardcase said. "Just so he keeps lining my pockets, he can sleep with flowers for all I care."

Fargo had a yard to cover. He raised the scythe, the tip poised for a fatal strike. At that exact moment the rat-faced killer turned around.

7

For a span of heartbeats the two men faced one another, Skye Fargo with the scythe hiked overhead, Sam Lafferty with his eyes and mouth wide in surprise. Suddenly jerking backward, Lafferty swooped both hands to the polished butts of his Smith & Wessons. He was amazingly quick but not quite quick enough. Fargo brought the scythe flashing down with all his might. Like a sword shearing into a melon, the pointed tip sheared into Lafferty's right eye and lanced deep into his skull. Lafferty stiffened and grunted, the pistols he had started to draw sliding back into their holsters as his fingers went limp.

Fargo was afraid the gunman would holler. Clamping his other hand over Lafferty's mouth, he let go of the scythe to loop his right arm around the gunman's waist and haul him toward the tack room. Depositing the body in a corner, he armed himself with the revolvers, sliding them under his shirt and covering them. Then he hurried out and took his seat on the bale, placing his arms behind him to give the impression they were still tied.

The Chemehuevi woman had not moved or made a sound. Fargo smiled and asked quietly, "Do you speak the white man's tongue?" Her blank expression was his answer. "Take the tray on back," he said, nodding at it for emphasis. She misunderstood, set it down, and filled the glass. Holding it in both hands, she raised it to his lips. To oblige her he drank, one eye over her shoulder for sign of the guards or anyone else. The liquid was cold lemon tea with a sugary taste, too sugary for his liking. Finishing, he again nodded at the tray, then at the doorway.

The young woman got his meaning. Touching his cheek, she said something in her own language. Neither of the guards tried to stop her as she calmly departed with her burden. But after about thirty seconds one of them stepped inside and scanned the interior. "Didn't I see that runt Lafferty come in with the squaw?"

Fargo feigned innocence. "Who?"

"You know. One of the two men who caught you." The man scratched his temple and stepped to the wide aisle between the stalls. "Where did he get to?"

"The only one I saw was the woman," Fargo said.

"Something ain't right," the guard declared. "Jim!" he called out. "Get your lazy backside in here."

The second man obeyed, his hand on his six-gun in anticipation of trouble. A scarecrow in loose-fitting clothes, he swung his cleft chin from side to side. "What's the matter, Hank?"

"I could have sworn Sam Lafferty brought that squaw over from the house, yet she just left alone. Now I don't see him anywhere." Hank nodded at Fargo. "Keep our friend there covered while I check around."

"Will do," Jim said, idly surveying the stable. He started to draw his revolver, then froze, eyes riveted to a particular spot on the floor. "Hey. What are those?" Darting over, he hunkered and brushed his fingertips over some crimson drops. "It's blood, or I'm a Chinaman!"

Fargo did not move or do anything else to draw attention to himself. The gambit paid off, for the two gunmen had momentarily forgotten about him. When Hank ran to his friend's side and bent to inspect the drops, Fargo slid his hands under his buckskin shirt and palmed the Smith & Wessons. Standing, he circled behind the pair, who had no idea they been played for jackasses until they heard the twin clicks of the pistol hammers being curled back. Instantly they spun. Jim imitated a tree but Hank dropped his hand toward his revolver. "Touch it and you're dead," Fargo said flatly.

The gun shark's fingers stopped a fraction of an inch above his Remington. "Damn you!" he fumed. "The boss will have our hides for letting you get the drop on us."

"Which would you rather have happen?" Fargo asked. "Be chewed out by Cutler, or be pushing up clover?" Not giving them time to mull it over, he indicated the tack room. "Back on in there. And keep your hands where I can see them or riling your boss will be the least of your worries."

Hank glared, Jim pouted, but they did as they were instructed, both elevating their arms above their shoulders. As they entered the room Jim sidestepped to avoid a bridle someone had left lying on the floor. The gunman started, then poked his friend. "I've found the runt."

"Sweet Jesus!" Hank exclaimed. "What is that you used on him, mister? A weed cutter?"

"Bad weeds come in all shapes and sizes," Fargo quipped, staying in the doorway so he could take cover right away should they resort to their hardware. They had done everything he wanted, but that might change now that they had seen Lafferty. "Shuck the hardware and turn around."

"So you can plug us in the back? Like hell," Hank said.

"Go ahead and shoot," Jim added. "You might nail both of us but our pards will hear the shot and come a-running. They'll get you for sure."

That they would, unless Fargo could prevail on the pair to do exactly as he wanted. "I won't shoot you if you do as I ask."

Hank's laugh was as brittle as eggshells. "And you expect us to believe you after what you've done to the runt? How stupid do you think we are?"

"How stupid do you think I am?" Fargo retorted. "I don't want any gunplay. All I'm interested in is getting out of here alive." Nodding at the halters, reins, and whatnot that hung on the wall, he said, "I'll even let you tie each other up, if that will make you feel safer." Impatience gnawed at his nerves like termites gnawing on wood. Every second of delay compounded the risk of being caught. "It's either that, or go for your guns. But I guarantee I'll put a slug into both of you before you clear leather."

Jim was the more sensible of the duo. "Sounds fair enough," he said, lowering a hand to his belt buckle. "Besides, what choice do we have? I like breathing."

"I don't trust him," Hank protested. "What's to stop him from taking that weed cutter to us once we're hogtied?"

"You have my word," Fargo said.

The gunhands exchanged looks. Jim shrugged and unbuckled his gunbelt, letting it fall with a thud. Hank balked, suspicion and dread inspiring him to crouch with his right hand curled.

"Go ahead." Fargo trained both revolvers on the gunman's face. "Your friend can wipe your brains off the walls and give you a proper burial later on. Maybe add a headstone that reads, 'Here lies a man who was too dumb to know when he was well off.'"

Jim placed a hand on his partner's arm. "Please, Hank. Listen to him. He didn't kill Sam and Rufus and Corncob Bob after they were knocked out, did he? I say we take a chance and do as he wants. If he goes for that weed cutter we can always scream our lungs out."

Hank muttered and uncoiled, then angrily undid his gunbelt and bent his knees to place in on the ground. "I must have been kicked in the head by a mule when I was a sprout to go along with this. But there, mister." Shoving his hardware away, he warily straightened. "Now what?"

"Tie yourselves up. Good and tight."

True to form, Hank hemmed and hawed, and they did it at a snail's pace, but presently both men were bound hand and foot. Hank's eyes did not leave Fargo as he stepped to a bin over which a number of cloth rags had been draped, rags used to clean the harness and saddles. Wedging the Smith & Wessons under his belt, he selected two of the rags and moved in front of Hank.

"What are those for?"

"Gags."

"The hell you say!" Hank declared. "If you think—"

Lunging, Fargo clamped a hand on the back of the gunman's head while simultaneously shoving the gag into his open mouth. Hank sputtered and thrashed, trying to spit the gag out, but Fargo jammed it in until the cutthroat's cheeks bulged like a chipmunk's. "That should keep you quiet a spell." He turned to Jim, who obligingly yawned his mouth wide and did not resist as the gag was inserted.

Fargo went to the corner where Lafferty lay. He heard Hank groan and sigh as he leaned down and removed cartridges from Lafferty's gunbelt and stuffed them into his pockets. He would much rather have his own pistol and the Henry but he had no idea where they had gotten to.

Emerging from the room, he glided to the doorway and peeked out. Little had changed. The Paiute men were still working, the women were filing back out to the fields. The gunhands at the corral had wearied of attempting to break the stubborn sorrel and were lounging against the rails, jawing. Fargo glanced toward the mansion. The Ovaro was still at the hitching post. He sorely desired to try and reach it but to do so would be surefire suicide. Seven or eight hardcases were in the vicinity of the porch and others were not far off. He'd be cut down before he got halfway.

He also wanted his own Colt, the Henry, and the toothpick. None of which he knew where to find. Quay might still have the knife but Pike's lieutenant was nowhere in sight. Circumstances being what they were, he had to make do with the Smith & Wessons for the time being. And with a different mount.

Three of the stalls were occupied. One by a dun, another by a mare so close to giving birth it would not do to ride her, the third by a fine palomino, or buttermilk horse as cowboys often called them. Fargo guessed the latter belonged to Pike Cutler. Palominos were as rare as hen's teeth in that part of the country and cost a lot more than the average animal.

The buttermilk pricked it ears and snorted but did not shy when Fargo slowly walked over. Patting its neck, he talked softly until the horse was accustomed to him. Then he threw on a blanket and saddle from among those that hung over the tops of the stalls and climbed on.

The Chemehuevi women were almost to the horse pasture. One of the gunnies from the corral was on his way to the long low building that must be their bunkhouse. The

Paiute men working on the new structure had stopped and were being given water.

Fargo visualized the layout of the valley in his mind's eye. East of the stable was the river and beyond it a thick belt of forest. Drawing one of the Smith & Wessons, he curled back the hammer, gripped the reins securely, and applied his spurs.

The palomino hurtled out of the stable as if shot from a cannon. Instantly, Fargo reined to the left. He was almost to the near corner when the first shout rang out. A chorus of angry yells and oaths rose as he cut around the corner, bearing eastward. A pistol cracked, the slug smacking into a plant within a foot of his elbow. Twisting, he saw the gunman who had left the corral, taking better aim. Firing from the waist, Fargo nailed the underling squarely in the chest. Other shots thundered, but not for long.

Out of the mansion barreled Pike Cutler. For someone so huge he could move with uncanny speed when he wanted. "Stop firing!" he bellowed loud enough to be heard in Salt Lake City. Immediately, every last gunman did. It was added proof, as if any were needed, of his sway over them, of the fear in which he was held by men who normally were afraid of nothing on earth. "So help me, I'll skin anyone alive who hits Napoleon! Mount up and get after them!"

The buttermilk horse was named Napoleon? Fargo could not help wryly musing as he raced hell-for-leather toward the river. Not having had much formal schooling, he would be the first to admit that he knew more about the mating habits of eagles than he did about world history. But everyone had heard of the cocky French dictator who set himself up as an emperor and ruled with an iron thumb. It was an added clue to Cutler's character, to his vanity.

Gunhands were sprinting toward the pasture. Others were mounting horses left near the mansion. A few were already in pursuit. They had automatically unlimbered their hardware but they did not cut loose.

The river was waist deep close to the bank. Fargo spurred the palomino into the water without a moment's hesitation. The horse responded superbly. It was an exceptional animal, almost as fine as the Ovaro. Surging in deeper, Fargo was careful to note how high it rose to avoid getting the Smith & Wessons wet.

Yips and hollers heralded a general rush of gunhands who had joined the chase, many riding bareback. The three who had been the first to do so were nearing the river. One happened to be Rufus.

Suddenly the palomino sank in almost to its shoulders. Fargo had blundered into a deep pool. Hauling on the reins, he skirted the hole, feeling his legs and upper thighs become drenched. By pushing against the saddle horn he raised his body high enough to avoid soaking his pockets— and the spare ammunition. As the far bank grew closer he spied a well-used trail.

Rufus had taken the lead. In his left hand was a rifle but he did not employ it. "What did you do to my pard?" he shouted. "How'd you get past Lafferty?"

Fargo did not answer. Why push his luck? Should Rufus learn Lafferty's fate, he might open fire. Cutler's wishes would not amount to a hill of beans to a man whose best friend had just been slain. Gaining the opposite side, Fargo goaded the buttermilk up a slippery bank onto solid ground. Ten or twelve badmen were crossing the grassy tract to the river. Rufus was halfway across, the other two doing their best to keep up.

Pike Cutler had not left the porch. Huge hands on his broad hips, he observed the chase with the calm demeanor of someone who was supremely confident of the outcome. Fargo could not be sure, but Cutler's mouth appeared to be curled in a mocking smile. For some reason Cutler was awful sure he could not get away, and that bothered him. It bothered him a lot.

With a toss of his head Fargo sped into the trees. Plenty of tracks testified that the trail was routinely used, probably by Chemehuevi work crews sent in for timber. He urged the palomino into a breakneck race for freedom. Or at least that was the impression he wanted to give to those who were after him.

Ahead was a bend. Fargo flew around it, his eyes glued

to his back trail. Consequently, he did not realize anyone was in front of him until a startled oath fell on his ears. Two of Cutler's gunhands were on their way back from whatever errand Cutler had sent them on. They had not been present when Fargo had made his break. They had not heard Cutler order the rest to hold their fire. So on seeing a stranger streak toward them on Cutler's personal mount, they jumped to the only logical conclusion. Fargo had stolen it and must be stopped.

On the right was a Mexican who was partial to a pair of Allen & Wheelock .44 army revolvers, on the left a tall drink of water who wore what looked to be a Manhattan six-inch-barreled navy pistol on his left hip. In unison they stabbed for their handguns, and their quickness was a credit to Cutler's choice of underlings.

Fargo swept the Smith & Wessons up and out. He fired a split second before they did, hot lead smashing into the Mexican's sternum and lifting the wiry cutthroat clear of the saddle. As for the other gunman, he was cored in the shoulder, the impact twisting him sharply but not unhorsing him. Recovering mere yards from the palomino, he gamely extended the Manhattan and sought to blow the top of Fargo's head off. Fargo's slug scored first, punching the badman in the jaw and flipping him into the vegetation.

The gunplay had taken mere seconds, but Fargo had slowed drastically to steady his aim and had lost valuable ground to the pack of human wolves who were after him. A glance showed Rufus coming around the bend with the other two not far behind. Shoving the Smith & Wessons under his belt, Fargo grabbed the reins and prepared to gallop off. By sheer happenstance, the Mexican's mount picked that moment to veer across the path, directly in front of the buttermilk.

Fargo wrenched on the reins in a frantic bid to avoid a collision. It was too late. The palomino slammed into the other horse like a bull buffalo gone amok and both horses lost their footing. Fargo was pitched forward. Before he could grab the saddle horn or the pommel, he felt himself leaving the saddle. In a rush of air the ground flashed toward his face.

8

At the last possible moment Skye Fargo tucked at the waist. Hitting on his shoulders, he rolled, his momentum carrying him a dozen feet to wind up sprawled on his back at the forest's edge. Scrambling to his knees, he saw Rufus bearing down on him holding the rifle by the barrel as if it were a club. He ducked just in time. The stock whooshed over his head, brushing his hat and nearly knocking it off. As Rufus's horse pounded past him, he rose and pivoted, bringing up the Smith & Wessons.

The din of hammering hooves behind him prevented him from firing. Fargo whirled and saw the other two side by side, intent on riding him down. He leaped to the right but not quite far enough. One of the horses clipped him and sent him tumbling into high weeds. Shaky and aching, he pushed to his feet.

The three gunmen had wheeled and were heading toward him in a compact line. All three had guns trained on him. It was as plain as the wicked glee that lit their faces that they would love to fill him with enough lead to sink a barge. They had him dead to rights. If he fired and dropped one the others were bound to return the favor, Cutler notwithstanding.

Aid came from an unlikely source. The palomino had risen shakily after its fall and was beside the trail, snorting and stomping its forelegs. Suddenly, as if it had a powerful hankering to return to the stable, it bolted between Fargo and the three gunmen. Seizing the opportunity, Fargo took a bound and flung himself at the saddle. He had to hook an arm around the saddle horn since he had revolvers in both hands. For precarious heartbeats gravity threatened to spill him to the ground but he clung on, whipped a leg up and over, and was spirited out of there with the palomino's flying mane tickling his face.

"Catch him!" Rufus bawled.

Lowering his boots, Fargo hooked them in the stirrups. He shoved one of the pistols into his holster to free a hand as he tore on around the bend. Any sense of elation he might have felt was eclipsed by consternation at seeing a motley knot of hardcases hurrying toward him. They whooped and brandished their weapons.

Fargo was boxed between the proverbial rock and a hard place. Behind him, Rufus and two coyotes. In front, more sidewinders than he could shake a stick at. They had him at their mercy, or so they assumed until he reined to the left and plunged into the woods. In long loping strides the palomino threaded through the trees, jumping a log that materialized underfoot. To discourage the gunhands and slow them down, Fargo snapped a couple of shots at the trail. Predictably, most scattered.

Rufus was not one of them. With bulldog persistence he clung to Fargo like glue, never falling more than fifteen feet behind. Thanks to the dense growth the palomino could not run flat out, allowing Rufus's animal to keep it in sight.

Fargo had to shake the gunman, somehow. He tried weaving and winding. He tried riding into the heaviest brush, into closely packed clusters of trees. He rode under dangerously low branches, hoping Rufus would be taken unawares. He tried grabbing limbs and bending them as he rode past, then letting go so they whipped back. But Rufus was too smart for him. Nothing Fargo tried worked.

The other two, though, had fallen behind and were no longer visible.

An insane idea occurred to Fargo, a ruse born of desperation and urgency. Wedging the second Smith & Wesson under his gunbelt, he scoured the woodland ahead. When a wide low limb appeared, he was ready. Shoving up off the buttermilk, he flung himself across it, wrapping both arms securely around it to keep from falling. Swiftly, he squatted and rotated, balancing precariously with one hand under him for support.

Rufus had seen what he had done. But with only seventeen or eighteen feet separating them, he could not bring his horse to a stop in time.

Fargo launched himself as if shot from a bow. Both arms rigid, he smashed into the gunman like a living battering ram. Rufus was bowled from the saddle, and together they toppled to the grass. Fargo contrived to be on top, his knees gouging into Rufus's stomach. Rufus went all red in the face, sputtering and gasping like a fish out of water. Vainly, Rufus tried to swing a fist but Fargo beat him to the punch. Literally. A right cross rendered Rufus unconscious.

Heaving upright, Fargo discovered both horses had run off. Crackling undergrowth warned him that the other hardcases would be there in a few moments. Grasping Rufus by the shoulders, Fargo dragged him into a thicket, then flattened. No sooner had he done so than the pair who had been with Rufus hastened on past. Soon the whole pack appeared, following them.

Fargo smiled grimly. With any luck the palomino would lead them a merry chase, buying him the time he needed. Rising, he took Rufus's Remington and stuffed it under his belt. A man could never have enough pistols when outnumbered twenty to one or better. He searched briefly for the rifle, which had gone flying when Rufus toppled, but it had vanished.

Rubbing a sore elbow, Fargo headed for the river. His plan was to hide out until nightfall. In under fifteen minutes he came to the trail and looked both ways before dashing across. To the north there were occasional yells and once a pistol cracked four times in succession. A signal, he reckoned. Maybe the palomino had been found.

When he was a score of yards into the brush he heard hooves pound on the trail. Someone was on their way back to the mansion. Possibly one of the searchers with a message for Cutler.

In due course Fargo reached the verdant growth that bordered the river. Climbing a willow to a convenient fork, he spied a lot of activity near the mansion. What it signified he did not know. Then half a dozen riders trotted toward the spot where he had crossed, and with them were a dozen Chemehuevi men. Trackers, Fargo deduced. Being used to hunt him down. He was not overly worried. The gunmen would take the Paiutes to the palomino, well away from where he had started out on foot.

Sunset was a good four hours off. Fargo made himself as comfortable as he could, sitting crosswise, his legs dangling. Over an hour dragged by, quiet minutes where the only event of note was a racket near the stable. His best guess was that Lafferty and the two guards had been found. Lafferty's death was bound to stir up the gunmen. They would crave revenge at any cost.

Another hour or so elapsed. Fargo grew drowsy despite his best efforts not to. His eyelids drooped regularly, and he had to shake himself to stay fully awake. He had just straightened for the umpteenth time when a vague feeling that he was no longer alone caused him to turn toward the trail. Stalking silently out of the greenery were three Chemehuevis. They had their eyes to the ground, reading sign, *his* sign. It would lead them right to the willow tree. Easing a Smith & Wesson out, he waited for the inevitable to happen.

One of the Chemehuevis uncurled, and Fargo was surprised to see it was the strapping young man he had seen earlier, chopping wood. The trio consulted, the muscular one pointing at bent blades of grass and then at the river.

Would they think he had crossed over? Fargo hoped. It was dashed when they bent to the spoor again and made a beeline for the tree. They were a stone's throw from the trunk when the vegetation crackled to the passage of horses and riders and onto the scene trotted Lucius Quay, Rufus and five other hardcases. Reining up, Quay addressed the strapping Paiute. "What the hell is taking so long, Hastina? I thought you were supposed to be the best tracker in your tribe."

"I am," the strapping Chemehuevi replied matter-of-factly.

"Then where did that son of a gun get to?" Quay demanded.

Hastina turned. His gaze roved to the willow and up it to the fork where Fargo roosted. Once again their eyes met. Hastina did not bend his head back or otherwise do anything that would give Quay an inkling of how close Fargo was. The corners of his mouth tweaked upward. Then he said in halting English, "Man in buckskins go into water. Him swim to other side, maybe."

"Into the river? Smart bastard. I wouldn't put it past him to swim on down past the spread to throw us off the scent." Quay adjusted his bowler. "Smart fella we're dealing with, boys. If I could recollect who he is, I'd die a happy man."

"Him leave little sign," Hastina said. "Part Indian, I think. Hard to trail."

"Trail?" Lucius Quay repeated, his brow knitting.

"Hard man to trail," the Chemehuevi stressed, apparently unsure whether Quay had understood.

"Yes. I suppose he would be." Waving an arm, Quay wheeled his mount. "Back to the house, gents. We'll tell Pike what we've learned and see what he wants to do." Thrusting a finger at the three Paiutes, he barked, "That includes you Injuns. Get in front of us. I don't like turning my back to heathens if I can help it."

Hastina's gaze roved to the fork of the willow and he gave a barely perceptible nod. Fargo grinned, then watched the searchers fade into the forest. He was in Hastina's debt. The Chemehuevi could have sealed his doom by giving him away, yet hadn't. The best way to repay the favor was to break the shackles of slavery the tribe suffered. To that end, he settled down to await the descent of darkness.

Stars speckled the heavens when Fargo shimmied to the ground. Hugging the riverbank, he jogged northward seeking a different place to ford. In a quarter of a mile he came to a likely spot. A finger of land jutted a third of the way into the water and was linked to a gravel bar by a ridge of partially submerged boulders. Once on the bar, he was confronted by a five-foot gap of deep water that lapped at the base of a modest slope.

Backing up, Fargo tucked his knees and girded himself. Five feet was not much, but a single misstep would plunge him in the river. Focusing on a tuft of grass at the bottom of the slope, he galvanized his legs into action. At the end of the gravel bar he threw himself upward, windmilling his arms and legs for added distance. The surface of the water blended into the dark, giving him the impression that he hung suspended in midair over a vast abyss. He braced his legs as he alighted but his weight was off center and his body was thrown backward as if by a phantom hand. Digging in his heels, he checked his fall.

Bent low, Fargo climbed. He was north of the pasture. Some of the horses were near the fence, betraying no fear as he moved along it to the rutted main trail. No hooves resounded in the night. By that he gathered no riders were abroad, which he thought strange. Even allowing for the men Cutler must have out hunting for him, there should be some around.

Warily, Fargo glided the length of the narrow strip of grass fringing the fence and road. Crouching at the corner post, he debated his next step. Many of the mansion's windows were aglow with light. The same with the bunkhouse. But the stable was dark, the corral shrouded by its starlit shadow. Not one hardcase roamed the grounds, leading Fargo to conclude it was their supper hour. He rose to go on, then promptly ducked down again when four men on horseback came around the southwest corner of the stable and angled toward the pasture.

Thinking they had seen him, Fargo dropped onto his stomach and snaked under the lowest rail. Drawing the Smith & Wessons, he aimed at the vague bulks that defined the riders. They were not in any hurry. Their voices reached him before they did.

" . . . why Quay made me go. I put in a full day guardin' those stinking Injuns."

"So did I, Barrett, but you don't hear me complaining. Quit your bellyaching and make do. Morning will come before you know it. Getting tomorrow off is worth having to stay up all night, in my book."

"Not in mine," commented a third man. "I'll be so tired, I'll sleep the day away."

"So what?" chimed in the fourth. "What else is there to do around here? Cutler won't let us touch those Digger gals. As if anyone will take him up on his offer and travel all the way here to buy them. California is a far piece, I tell you."

The first man snorted. "Not so far that it wouldn't be worth someone's while. Figure it out yourself. Pike is offerin' thirty prime Injun gals at a hundred dollars a head. That sounds like a lot until you take into account that each will earn that much in a month. I ain't no great shucks at arithmetic, but I know a good deal when I hear one. If I had the money, I'd buy 'em my own self."

Fargo was startled by the news. Cutler was selling the Paiute maidens to anyone who met his price. Imagining the use they would be put to filled him with simmering fury. It was all well and good for a woman to choose to be a dove, but it was another story entirely when timid sorts like the Chemehuevis were forced to sell their bodies. Most wouldn't last a year. Despair and disease would reap a ferocious toll. The few who did not succumb would live on in unending misery, wishing they had joined their sisters.

The quartet were almost abreast of the fence. Fargo placed his cheek to the soil as one of the foursome spouted off.

"It won't be so bad tonight. All we have to do is keep our eyes skinned in case that feller tries to get out of the valley."

"Oh, is that all? And what if he sneaks up on you and slits your stupid throat? Remember what he did to Lafferty. Me, I ain't sleepin' a wink."

"Did you hear what Rufus said? He's going to carve that hombre into tiny pieces and scatter them for the buzzards. And he doesn't care what Pike does."

"Big talk. I'd like to—"

The men goaded their horses into a trot, drowning out their conversation. Fargo did not stir until they were long gone. Sliding under the rail, he stood and probed the night for more gunmen. Rowdy laughter and the faint clank of a pot verified that the majority of Cutler's gang were eating. He pulled his hat brim low and sped toward the building under construction. It was nearest, and from it he could see the mansion clearly.

The last Fargo knew, the Ovaro had been tied to the hitching post in front, so that was where he would look first. Because one way or another, he was not leaving Red Valley without the stallion. His Colt could always be replaced. A new Henry could be purchased in Salt Lake City. An Arkansas toothpick was available from most any knife maker. But the pinto was one of a kind. It had been his dependable companion on treks as far east as Florida, as far north as Canada, as far south as Mexico. He would sooner part with an arm than give it up.

Hunkered behind a stack of lumber, Fargo scoured the yard and frowned. The hitching post was empty. So was the corral. The only place left to check was the stable. Without hesitation he bolted toward it, his skin prickling at the thought of being gunned down in the open. Comforting darkness swallowed him as he entered. He paused to let his eyes adjust. A splotch of white in the foremost stall drew him inward, and a welcoming nicker greeted him. "Did you think I'd forget you?" he whispered.

The pinto nuzzled him. Fargo stroked it a few times, then roved along the stall hunting for his saddle. For once things went his way. It was close by, along with his saddle blanket and his saddlebags. In the remote recesses of his brain a tiny voice blared a warning. Something was wrong, terribly wrong. It had all been too easy. But since it was too late to turn back, he gripped the saddle blanket and turned to throw it on the Ovaro.

"Now!"

At the imperious command, matches flared on all sides. Half a dozen lanterns were lit at once. Their stark glow bathed the stalls and the center aisle, catching Fargo in their bright glare. Ten hawkish faces gleamed with vicious triumph. Gun barrels glistened dully. From the rear of the hay bales strode an imposing man mountain whose smile reeked of cunning and brutality.

"Mr. Fargo. We meet again," Pike Cutler said. "How nice of you to change your mind and accept my gracious hospitality."

9

Skye Fargo strolled into The Bull's Head and knew right away he was in for a rough night. A luscious redhead, a curvaceous blonde, and a brunette whose melons heaved against her tight green dress with every breath she took, converged and grabbed hold of him. They looked at one another. Then the redhead yanked on his right arm, saying, "He's mine! I saw him first!" "No, you didn't!" challenged the blonde as she hauled on his other arm. "I did." The brunette clutched his shirt. Suddenly twisting, she nearly threw him to the hard floor. "You're both wrong!" she squealed. "He's mine!" They commenced to pull and tug so fiercely that his arms were not only torn from his sockets, they were ripped clean off. The blonde brandished his right one as if it were a flag, saying, "Forget it! He's busted! I don't want him now." But the other two would not relent. They shook him so vigorously, his teeth chattered.

Fargo realized it was a dream at the same instant he realized someone really was shaking him. Blinking, he squinted up into the snarling visage of Rufus. "What do you want?" he asked, his tongue feeling as if it were covered with coarse cloth. He was on his back on a small pile of straw in the stable, exactly where the hardcases had left him the night before. His wrists weren't bound, but this time he was chained by the waist to one of the beams that held up the loft. He recalled that Pike Cutler had promised to send for him first thing in the morning, and outside a telltale pink flush framed the eastern horizon. "Is it time to see your boss?"

"No," Rufus sneered. "It's time for you to try and escape again."

"What?" Befuddled by sleep, Fargo sluggishly sat up.

"You heard me, you rotten scum." Rufus rose and flourished a long key. The same key Lucius Quay had used to lock the padlock that held the five-foot chain to the beam. Stepping to the lock, he quickly inserted the key and twisted. The lock popped open with a distinct click. "Go ahead. Escape."

For a few seconds Fargo wondered if it was another dream. Then Rufus dropped the key and circled around him to retrieve the pitchfork. "I happened to be up and about and came by just as you freed yourself." Halting between Fargo and the entrance, Rufus showed his yellow teeth in a sinister smile. "I tried my best not to hurt you but you put up a hell of a fight. So I was forced to run you through." To demonstrate, he lunged, thrusting the tines at Fargo's midsection.

Only an adroit sidestep saved Fargo from grave harm, or much worse. The chain looped tight around his waist clanked as he moved, and he pried at the links to get it off. His mind was crystal clear now. Vividly he recalled what one of the four riders had mentioned the previous night: "Did you hear what Rufus said? He's going to carve that hombre into tiny pieces and scatter them for the buzzards. And he doesn't care what Pike does."

"Sam Lafferty was my pard," Rufus now declared. "We rode together for nigh on eight years. Maybe he was no-account to some, but he was my best friend. And I aim to plant you just like you planted him."

"Your boss won't like it," Fargo stalled while pushing at the stubborn links.

"Can't be helped," Rufus stated. "There are some things a man has to do if he's to go on claiming to be a man. I'll take my medicine, whatever it might be. And it'll be worth it because I'll know Lafferty is resting easier in his grave."

"He's dead. He doesn't care one way or the other what happens." For the life of him, Fargo could not unravel the chain. Over three feet of it dangled down to his knees, slapping against them every time he jerked at the links encircling his waist.

"Where does it say dead folks don't have feelings?" Rufus countered. "They shed their bodies, is all. My ma told me all about it when I was a kid. And you're about to find out for yourself that she was right." So saying, Rufus growled like a panther and streaked the pitchfork up and out as if it were a Cheyenne lance.

Fargo was inspecting the chain to learn why it would not loosen. He knew not to take his eyes off an enemy but he needed the damn chain off. By pure chance he raised his head as Rufus attacked. The four dung-encrusted tines speared at his neck, missing by a whisker when he threw himself to the left.

"How's it feel having the shoe on the other foot?" Rufus taunted. "When I'm done with you, your body will look like a sieve. You'll be spouting blood like one of those fancy fountains in New Orleans."

Fargo didn't doubt it. The tines were long and slightly curved and sharp enough to pierce him through. He skipped aside to evade another thrust.

"I'll be famous after I kill you," Rufus said. "Folks everywhere will hear of it. Why, they might write it up in one of those penny storybooks, with pictures and all."

Fargo had no idea what the killer was raving about. He had more important considerations, such as staying alive, for starters. Dodging and ducking, he avoided the pitchfork again and again.

"Stand still, damn your bones!" Rufus protested. "You're worse than a jackrabbit, the way you hop around."

Did the gunman seriously think he would meekly let himself be slaughtered? Fargo marveled as he bounded toward the wide doorway. Others might be up. If he could raise a ruckus, it would bring them on the run. But he took only a couple of strides when the chain banged against his left knee, spiking raw pain up his leg. He nearly fell. Tottering, he backpedaled away from Rufus, who stormed at him like a human hurricane, swinging the pitchfork in a sizzling pattern of imminent death.

"Now I've got you!"

Fargo backed into a stall and had nowhere to go. Cornered, he gripped the chain with both hands, close to his body, and when Rufus drove the tines at his chest, he shifted and swung the chain as if it were a whip. It wrapped around the pitchfork's handle, wrapped good and fast. Wrenching mightily, Fargo sough to tear the pitchfork from Rufus's grasp but Rufus held on.

Straining and heaving, neither could gain the upper hand. Fargo threw all his strength into a turn to the right but the chain would not budge. Rufus tilted the handle, then abruptly moved in close and delivered a kick to Fargo's shins. Torment inflamed Fargo's leg. Limping badly, he jerked on the chain again and again, like a man possessed. But it was no use.

The impasse was resolved by accident. In their constant turning and twisting, they had moved near to the hay bales. Fargo did not take note of them until he violently bumped into the one he had sat on the day before. Upending, he fell, and his weight succeeded in doing what brute force alone could not. The pitchfork was torn from Rufus's hands. It fell onto the bale, then clattered to the ground at Fargo's side. He snatched at it, but as he did, Rufus leaped and grabbed the handle, too. Grappling for control, they rolled back and forth.

Fargo slammed into the high stack of bales and could not move. Pinned, he exerted his corded sinews to their utmost and almost threw Rufus off. Almost, but not quite. Agleam with bloodlust, Rufus stiffened his iron arms and pressed down for all he was worth. Inch by gradual inch the horizontal handle lowered toward Fargo, toward his exposed throat. He felt it touch his skin. The contact motivated him to buck upward but he could not toss the gunman off.

"You're mine now!" Rufus gloated.

The smooth handle gouged into Fargo's neck. Bitterly, he struggled, but his adversary had the advantage. The wood gouged deeper, steadily deeper, on the verge of choking off his breath, of crushing his larynx. He resisted strenuously but he could not brace his elbows under him for the added purchase he needed.

Agony racked his throat. Fargo found it difficult to breathe. Of all the ways he had imagined meeting his end, none had been like this. He'd always hoped it would be quick and painless. In a gunfight, perhaps. Or jumped by a grizzly and ripped apart before he could lift a finger in his defense.

"Die!" Rufus hissed in wolfish glee. Then he did a strange thing. He unexpectedly slackened his grip and slumped forward.

Fargo surged up off the ground, flinging Rufus from him. He retained his grip on the pitchfork and elevated it to drive the tines into the killer's torso. But he never followed through. For at that moment the tingle of cold steel being pressed against his temple froze him in place.

"No need for that, friend. I walloped him so hard, he'll be out for hours." Lucius Quay stepped into view, moving back several paces. In the entrance were four more cutthroats, their hardware conspicuous. "Drop it," he directed.

Fargo cast the pitchfork down, sat on the bale, and rubbed his sore throat. "What kept you?" he croaked.

Chuckling, Quay said, "You're damned lucky I came when I did. Pike sent me to fetch you to breakfast." Rather sadly he regarded the prone form of the man he had knocked out. "The poor fool. Rufus should have left well enough alone. The last jackass who disobeyed wound up as maggot food." Gesturing at two of the gunmen, he told them, "Bind him, hand and foot, and put him in a stall. Mr. Cutler will be down to see him directly, I reckon."

Fargo groped the chain. Low down on his backside he found where it had become entangled with his gunbelt, probably when it was wrapped around him, explaining why he could not get shed of it. He did so now, and straightened.

"After you," Quay said.

A golden crown perched on the shoulders of the world. In the woodland birds sang in ritual chorus to welcome the new dawn. Across the river deer grazed. Red Valley was a pristine sanctuary for man and beast alike, a sanctuary violated by the vile spidery presence of Pike Cutler, whose spreading web of evil would soon transform the valley into a den of iniquity rivaled by few in the entire West.

A Chemehuevi woman dressed in a skimpy maid's uniform answered the door. Fargo was ushered down a plush wide corridor into a lavish dining room that fronted the rising sun. Already seated at the head of an ornate mahogany table was the master of the mansion, meticulous as always in an expensive suit, his imposing frame dwarfing the polished chair in which he reposed like a king on his throne.

"Good morning, Mr. Fargo. I trust you slept well enough in light of the circumstances."

It was a statement, not a question. "Except for the rude awakening I had—" Fargo began, and caught himself. "You know who I am."

"Thanks to Mr. Quay there, yes." Cutler nodded at his lieutenant, who stood in the doorway, pistol leveled. "He ran into you once, I hear. You beat him at cards rather handily, and he has resented it ever since." Cutler's glittering eyes scrutinized Fargo with renewed interest. "So you're the renowned Trailsman, the greatest scout since Daniel Boone, the man who can track an ant across solid rock, wrestle grizzlies into submission, and who rides whirlwinds for entertainment."

"Been hitting the bottle early, I take it?" Fargo said as he took a seat on the man mountain's left so he could see out an enormous window toward the river.

"Perhaps I exaggerate a trifle," Cutler conceded, smirking. "But it is rare that I have a guest of your caliber. Small wonder you managed to escape. I won't make the mistake of underestimating you a second time, you can believe me." Waving a slab of a hand at Quay, he said, "Your services are no longer needed, Lucius. Go about your business."

"But, boss, what if he tries to get away again?"

Pike Cutler's countenance grew as flinty as quartz. "Are you implying I would be unable to stop him?" Suddenly those demonic eyes narrowed. "Wait a second. What was that about a rude awakening?"

Lucius Quay coughed. "Rufus is to blame. He tried to run Fargo through with a pitchfork. I had the men hogtie him."

The massive would-be emperor of southern Utah reared out of his seat like a mammoth about to charge. "*Rufus did what?*" he grated through clenched teeth. Cutler was a volcano set to explode. His thick fingers gripped a spoon and wrapped tight, bending the metal like so much flax. With a Herculean visible effort he slowly composed himself, capping the emotional lava that steamed and boiled within him. "Keep him tied, then, Mr. Quay. Tomorrow evening he will be another object lesson for the men."

"How's that, boss?"

"You'll see." Cutler wagged his hand. "Leave us. My guest and I have a lot to discuss."

Fargo was amazed by the man's self-confidence. As usual, his host did not appear to be wearing a weapon. Now that they were alone, what was to stop him from grabbing a knife and ending his ordeal then and there? He thought about it. He fingered the two knives and selected the sharpest. But as he molded his hand to the hilt, two gunmen materialized outside the window, both bearing rifles. One waved to Cutler, who waved back.

"I think of everything, Mr. Fargo. Two more are stationed outside the front door, two more at the rear. Were you to indulge your fantasy, you would never leave my house alive."

Fargo slid his hand to his lap. "House? It's more like a palace." He was being sarcastic but Cutler smiled and gazed fondly around the regal room.

"Yes, isn't it. I can't tell you how hard I've worked to make my dream come true. Perhaps you would permit me to bore you with the particulars?"

"I already know the gist of it," Fargo said, and related the details he had gleaned so far. How Cutler intended to lay claim to more land than the largest spread in Texas. How Cutler was forming his own private little army. And how Cutler aimed to enslave the Chemehuevis and other tribes. "What I don't get," Fargo concluded, "is why you want to sell the Chemehuevi women. The men are bound to rise up if you do. They'll only take so much."

"You give them too much credit and me not enough." Cutler propped his elbows on the table and made a teepee of his hands. "I do not plan to enslave them, as you put it. Oh, for the moment they have their uses. My own men have a distaste for menial labor. But once the buildings are done and other projects completed, I will treat the Paiutes as I treat all insects who become a nuisance. I will wipe them off the face of the earth, every last man, woman, and child."

"And the other tribes in the region?"

"The same, once I'm ready to spread out. By this time next year there will not be an Indian alive south of Mount Dutton."

Fargo had suspected as much, but hearing it from Cutler's own mouth staggered him. The cost of lives would be fearsome. Hundreds—no thousands—would be sacrificed on the alter of Cutler's lust for power and wealth.

"You think I'm a monster, don't you?" the huge man asked. "Don't deny it. I can see it in your eyes." Cutler lifted a glass of juice and sipped. "But be fair. I'm doing no more or less than scores of ranchers have done before me. Arizona, New Mexico, Texas, you name a place where settlers haven't had to wage war against Indians."

"Fight them, yes. But not exterminate whole tribes," Fargo said with roiling passion. "Why not just drive them off their land and let it go at that?"

"Gnats breed more gnats. I don't want them making trouble for me later on. So I will do what the government has been saying we should all along." Cutler's tone lowered to a menacing rumble. "Mark my words, Mr. Fargo. I will brook no interference with my plans. Anyone who poses a threat faces the same fate."

Fargo was so incensed that he came close to throwing himself at Cutler. Instead, he changed the subject. "What about all those horses in the corral? No three of them wear the same brand."

Cutler leaned back. "My men have stolen them from isolated ranches to the north and from wagon trains bound for the Oregon Country. A few here, a few there, it all adds up. Over the next several months the brands will be altered and I'll sell them for thousands. Just as I'm selling the Paiute women." He oozed arrogance. "I've come a long way since Ohio."

"Is that where you were raised?" Fargo asked to ferret out more information.

"Yes, I'm sad to say. Early on I wearied of the simpletons who called themselves my family and friends. Farmers, for the most part. All they talked about was the weather and their crops and how much milk their cows were giving." Cutler paused. "It was nauseating."

"Did you hear about Red Valley back there?"

Cutler was staring into the distance but really staring backward in time. "Be sensible. How would I have?" He shook his great moon head. "No, I was seeking a spot like this, though. I had developed a master strategy to establish my own ranch by hook or by crook, as the saying goes." He grew wistful. "I was in Wyoming when I learned about this valley from an old mountain man who had befriended the Chemehuevis. He told me how he would like to come back and settle down here one day."

Fargo guessed the next development. "That's when you had a brainstorm."

"I prefer to call it inspiration," Cutler corrected him. "But yes, I saw Red Valley's true potential. Why settle for a ranch when I could carve out much more? The situation was ideal. No government to speak of, no law authorities to meddle, no army presence to contend with." His barrel of a chest swelled. "Red Valley has become the center of my growing empire, as I foresaw."

There was that word again. "Empire," Fargo said slowly. "And you named your horse Napoleon."

"It's no coincidence,'" Pike Cutler said. "I've long been fond of books, history books in particular. Early on I was fascinated by Bonaparte, by his genius, his daring, his courage. Call me childish if you will, but I flatter myself that he and I have a lot more in common than would seem apparent. My keenest regret is that I wasn't born several hundred years ago in Europe. Half the continent would have been under my sway."

Fargo had seldom heard such out-and-out nonsense. "So that's what this is all about? You want to be like some runt who went around with a hand up his shirt?"

Cutler adopted stony silence for a full minute. "I expect stupidity from my men since most never attended school. The only reason they do my bidding is to line their pockets. But I had hoped that you, at least, would better appreciate the goal I have set. We're both widely traveled, both intelligent, both survivors."

"And one of us is a cold-blooded butcher." Fargo did not mince words. "I don't know much about Napoleon, I'll admit, but I never heard tell that he killed women and children."

"You miss the grander design," Cutler said testily. "Certain sacrifices must be made, is all. Or, to phrase it in terms you can understand, the ends always justify the means."

"How does Bob Newton fit into the scheme of things?" Fargo remembered to ask.

"Corncob Bob and I met down in Texas. He's as dependable as the day is long. His trading post is my supply point, and it lets him act as my eyes and ears to the outside world. He alerted me that you were snooping around, and he'll do the same if any lawmen or a cavalry patrol should happen by." Cutler smoothed his jacket. "As I told you, I think of everything."

"So what now?"

"Nothing has changed since your escape attempt. Tomorrow evening we will hold our regular festivities. Within a month I expect word from California about the women. Once they're gone, I'll dispose of the rest of the tribe. The Washoes will be next, after they have worked themselves to the bone for me, like the Paiutes." Regarding Fargo intently, Cutler put both hands on the edge of the table. "Be totally honest. What do you think?"

"You're loco."

"Please. Be serious."

Fargo shook his head in disgust. The man was so fond of himself that he couldn't accept when others held an opinion contrary to his own. Cutler pictured himself as some sort of glorious conqueror when in truth and in fact he was a petty nobody willing to slaughter scores of innocents to carry out a warped scheme spawned by a sick mind. "I am serious. I feel sorry for you, mister. How old are you? Thirty? You've gone through half your life and still haven't learned the first thing about living."

"Gibberish," Cutler spat. "Spare me your feeble sympathy. Feel sorry for yourself, if you must feel sorry for anyone. Because tomorrow evening your illustrious career comes to an end."

Fargo was spared having to reply by the timely arrival of a Chemehuevi man in the garb of a butler. The clothes did not fit well, lending him the aspect of a bronzed scarecrow. Cutler ordered eggs and bacon and toast for the two of them, then launched into a detailed account of his wanderings.

Sipping coffee, Fargo listened with half an ear. The food came, but the eggs and bacon turned out to be the first of several courses. Cutler also downed five flapjacks smothered in syrup, half a loaf of fresh bread drowning in butter, a melon, and sugary rolls. Watching all that food go down was enough to give Fargo a stomach ache.

After the meal Cutler rambled on. How the man loved to hear himself talk! He crowed about his so-called empire, about the grand estate he would one day have, about running for political office years down the road.

Fargo tired of hearing him prattle on and flatly said so, adding, "If you want to talk me to death, do it some other time. I'd rather be chained up than have to listen to you jabber the day away."

Cutler was insulted. "Very well," he said rising. "You shall have your wish."

At the front door, Cutler said severely, "I can't say it's been a pleasure. I had high hopes you would be different from the rest, but you aren't. You're as crude and ignorant as most of your breed. For the life of me, I can't understand how you ever acquired the reputation you have." He offered his ponderous paw.

Fargo shook, just for the hell of it. Cutler's hand swallowed his, and granite fingers closed like a vise. In all his born days Fargo had never felt such inhuman power in another man, strength so staggering that Cutler could have crushed his hand like an eggshell. As it was, the man mountain squeezed hard enough to flare pain clear to his shoulder. Fargo hid it, though, refusing to give Cutler the satisfaction of feeling superior.

Two gunmen returned Fargo to the stable. They chained him to the beam and later gave him a blanket. From then until evening he was left alone. A different pair brought food and drink. Afterward he was allowed to stretch his legs.

Nightfall found him curled on the straw. He was comfortable enough, given the circumstances. From time to time he had heard rustling in one of the stalls, and a muffled angry voice. Rufus, he gathered, was still back there, and had been gagged as well as bound. No one brought water or food to Lafferty's former pard, or untied him so he could relieve himself.

The next day was Saturday. Shortly after sunup Lucius Quay brought coffee and more of those sugary rolls on a tray, then sat on a bale. "Today is the big day, Trailsman. This evening you get put to the test. The boys are laying ten to one odds against you, but I bet five dollars on you anyway. Just in case you're luckier than most."

"What kind of test?" Fargo inquired.

Quay snickered. "I'd hate to spoil the surprise. Wait until tonight. But if I were you, I'd eat everything we give you and try to nap this afternoon. Trust me. You need to be in top condition or you won't last five minutes." Quay glanced down the aisle. "Poor Rufus won't have a prayer. He doesn't get a lick of nourishment. Cutler's orders."

"Your boss is stark raving mad, you know."

"If he is, I'd give anything to be the same," Lucius Quay said half to himself. "Look at all he's accomplished. You've been in his mansion. Do madmen live in the lap of luxury like Cutler does? Do they get away with all he has and not get caught? No, Pike isn't mad. He's shrewd, maybe one of the shrewdest hombres who ever lived."

Fargo propped his back against the beam and swallowed some coffee. Like the rolls, it was laced with sugar. "You should have stuck to cards. Cutler has dealt you a bad hand, and you won't realize it until someone calls you."

"Spare me the advice. For once I'm hitched to a winner, and I'm going to see this through to the end."

The remainder of the day was quiet except for occasional outbursts from Rufus, who kicked the stall and hollered until he was hoarse. The guards ignored him.

Fargo tried to catch some sleep but couldn't. Twilight shrouded the valley when footfalls announced the arrival of Lucius Quay and six gunmen. "It's time!" Quay gaily exclaimed, producing the key to the heavy padlock.

"For what?" Fargo asked, not expecting an answer.

"For that gent you think is mad as a loon to beat you to death with his bare hands."

10

The grassy area in front of the mansion was ablaze with light. A large ring of lanterns lit up the front yard as brightly as day, while more were suspended from the pillars and others had been placed along the edge of the porch. Every last gunman in Cutler's small army was present, many drinking whiskey straight from bottles. They were laughing and joking and having a grand old time. Saturday night was the one night of the week Pike Cutler let them do pretty much as they pleased and they were making the most of it.

To Skye Fargo's surprise, the Chemehuevis were also there, the women huddled close together, the men standing to one side. At the forefront was Hastina, who raised a hand in greeting as Fargo was brought into the center of the circle by Lucius Quay and two badmen. The hubbub grew louder, some of the hardcases hooting and yipping.

"About time!" one yelled. "Now we can get this tea party under way!"

"Hey, Trailsman!" shouted another. "Ready to meet your Maker?"

The mocking mirth and rowdy voices suddenly stilled as Rufus was brought into the light by four cutthroats who marched him over next to Fargo. Rufus looked like hell. His face was pasty. Sweat poured from every pore. His clothes were rumpled and caked with straw and dirt. Nervously wringing his hands, he turned this way and that. "Jess! Harvey! Webber!" he croaked. "Howdy, boys!" No one responded and Rufus grew more agitated. "This can't mean what I think it does!" he bawled. "I'm your friend, damn it! You can't let him do this to me!"

Quay and the six gunmen joined the ring of somber killers. The flickering pale glow of the lanterns painted their faces in ghostly hues, as if they were a jury of cold wraiths standing in judgment on one of their own.

Rufus gestured. "Brice! You rode with Lafferty and me some time back, remember? Talk to him. Tell him I don't deserve this." The man appealed to might as well have been sculpted from stone. Clasping his hands in supplication, Rufus moved toward the somber ring. "In God's name, don't just stand there like that! Do something!"

Lucius Quay pointed his revolver, halting Rufus dead in his tracks. "Quit your blubbering, you fool. You've brought this on yourself. Now try to take your medicine like a man."

"But I don't want to die!" Rufus screeched.

"You should have though of that before you tried to kill Fargo," Quay said. "You know the rules as well as we do."

Rufus was practically in tears. Fear twisted his features as he rotated three hundred and sixty degrees, staring in mute appeal at each and every one of his former companions. He might as well have appealed to statues. Only one man bit a lip and averted his gaze. Rufus gave a convulsive shudder, exhaled loudly, and squared his shoulders. "So this is the way it is," he said so softly that only Fargo heard. "I reckon I should have known. Rattlers ain't to be trusted no how."

At that juncture the front door opened and out strolled Pike Cutler. Immaculate as always in a fine suit and shined shoes, he also had a large white towel draped over his bearish shoulders. His underlings parted to permit him to enter the circle. Eyes aglitter, he came to the center, towering over Fargo and Rufus. The latter retreated a few steps, swallowing hard. "Good evening, gentlemen," Cutler said amiably, and bobbed his huge head at the firmament. "Isn't it a fine night? I trust both of you will provide excellent entertainment."

"Call it what you want," Fargo said, "it's another name for murder."

Cutler balled up the towel and tossed it to Lucius Quay.

"I beg to differ. It's not as if you'll be gunned down in cold blood. Both of you can defend yourselves to the best of your ability. And if, by some miracle, you should win, you earn your freedom."

Some of the gunmen laughed.

Removing his jacket, Cutler neatly folded it and carried it over to set it at Quay's feet. His shirt was next, and an undershirt. Stripped to the waist, the man mountain turned. Never had Fargo seen so much muscle packed onto a single human being. Rippling layers covered Cutler's immense chest. His abdomen resembled a washboard, it had so many ridges and bumps of knotted sinew. As for his arms, they were as thick around as Fargo's thighs. The man was a colossus of raw power, a living, breathing titan, a human wall. "So? Which one of you cares to go first?"

Rufus gulped and cast anxiously about like a scared rabbit ready to bolt.

"I will," Fargo said.

Pike Cutler moved to the left and set himself, his giant hands balled into mallets. "Very well. Whenever you are ready. I only pray you will prove more of a challenge than most do. My mettle hasn't truly been tested in ages."

Fargo started to circle when suddenly, to his amazement, Rufus rushed between them and shoved him backward. "No! Let me. I'm sick and tired of kowtowing to this miserable son of a bitch. I was afraid there for a bit, but now I've come to my senses."

"How commendable," Cutler said suavely. "It seems that in all vermin there burns a spark of genuine courage."

Rufus motioned at the ring of hardened killers. "Did you hear that? You're riding for a man who thinks we're scum!"

Some of the gunmen glanced sharply at their employer.

"I never made any such claim," Cutler said, irritated. "You're bending my words to try and save yourself." Abruptly, with incredible quickness for someone so gigantic, he darted forward and flicked his right arm. It was a short jab, thrown almost casually, yet it rocked Rufus on his heels and sent him tottering into Fargo. "For that insult you will suffer. Suffer unbearably."

Fargo had grabbed Rufus to keep him from falling. The gunman shook his head to clear it, then worked his jaw. "Damn you, Pike!" he screamed, and threw himself at the giant in a frenzy.

Cutler never moved. He stood there as calmly as could be and let Rufus rain punches on his ribs and his stomach, and not once did he wince or flinch or show that the punches were having any effect whatsoever. It was as if Rufus were pounding on a block of marble. Dozens of blows he landed, and all he succeeded in doing was tiring himself out. At last, spent, Rufus backed away and sucked in deep breaths.

"Is that the best you can do?" Cutler scoffed. "Small wonder Fargo beat you and Lafferty at the trading post. I've been hit harder by a woman."

Blind rage drove Rufus at the giant again. A flurry of fists pommeled Cutler, who made an effort to only block punches thrown at his face. Rufus swung and swung and swung. He swung until his arms were leaden and he could not swing anymore. Then he bent over, exhausted, panting heavily, his knuckles cracked and bleeding. "I hope you rot in hell," he gasped out.

"Your first," Cutler said, and delivered an uppercut. A single sweep of his right arm, without putting his whole weight or heft into it, yet it lifted Rufus clear off the ground and spilled him onto his back in a disjointed heap.

When Rufus did not move, Fargo stepped over and sank onto a knee. He gave Rufus's shoulder a shake. The gunman's head flopped from side to side, empty eyes fixed on the sky. "His neck is broken. He's dead."

"What else did you expect?" Cutler said, straightening. "I have yet to meet my equal in personal combat. Pugilists, barroom toughs, waterfront ruffians, I've fought them all and always proved their better." Going to Quay, he took the towel and dabbed it at his chest and under his arms. "Remove the carrion. Bury him in the morning."

Two hardcases dragged Rufus from the circle toward the

stable. Many of his former friends stared thoughtfully at the miserable crumpled figure, and when they looked at Pike Cutler there was something new in their expressions. Something Cutler did not appear to notice, or else considered unimportant.

The man mountain walked to the middle again and adopted a boxing posture. "Now it is your turn, Trailsman. Try to put on a better show, if you don't mind. I get bored easily."

As Fargo stepped to the right he saw Hastina watching intently. The Chemehuevis had not uttered a sound the whole time. To them, the brutal spectacle must be yet another example of the white man's limitless bloodlust. "Did you mean what you said about earning my freedom if I win?"

Cutler acted offended. "No matter what else you may think of me, you must admit that I am a man of my word. But since you dare doubt . . ." He poked a thumb the size of an iron spike at Lucius Quay. "Should he prevail, you will return his weapons and his horse and permit him to leave Red Valley unharmed. Understood?"

"Whatever you say," Quay answered, but Fargo could tell that the former gambler did not like it.

"Now then," Cutler said. "Let us see if you have more grit than Rufus. Whenever you are ready, you may attack." Bending slightly at the knees, he waited, his chiseled physique reflecting the light like burnished metal.

Fargo was in no hurry. He had no intention of making the same mistakes Rufus had. Cautiously gliding to the right, he studied Cutler closely, searching for a weak spot. With some men it was their stomachs. Years of easy living turned their guts into flab. Cutler's, though, was rock hard. Other men had glass jaws, but somehow Fargo doubted it would be the case with Cutler. The man's jutting jawline hinted at bone thick enough to ward off any blow.

How about the knees? Fargo wondered. A good kick might bring Cutler toppling down. Then again, they might be as solid as the rest of him. Fargo halted, vaguely aware that a collective breath was being held by the onlookers.

Cutler's dark eyes were riveted to his like those of some great cat toying with a puny mouse.

"Sometime tonight would be nice."

Fargo feinted to the left, pretending to throw a hook, and Cutler moved an arm to block, leaving himself open to an uppercut. Levering his arm up and in, Fargo rammed his right fist onto the point of the giant's jaw. Any other man would have been jarred off his feet, or knocked unconscious. But all Pike Cutler did was blink. A single bat of the eyes. So much for the glass jaw notion. Fargo stepped back, his right hand throbbing, and pondered what to try next.

"Congratulations," the lord of Red Valley said. "I actually felt that. You're much stronger than most."

The compliment washed off Fargo like water off a duck's back. Scratching his chin as if perplexed, he saw Cutler gaze smugly toward Quay. In that brief instant when Cutler was distracted, Fargo glided in close and landed two punishing hits to Cutler's ribs, just below the left arm. Instantly he skipped out of reach of those massive hams Cutler called hands, one whisking by his cheek as he did.

Cutler frowned and bent his squat neck to look down at himself. "That stung a bit. Keep it up, though. This promises to be interesting. Perhaps I misjudged you. Maybe there is more to you than meets the eye."

Fargo resented being treated as if he were an insignificant bug. He danced in swiftly and just as swiftly danced back out when Cutler pumped a knobby fist at his face to keep him at bay. Fargo took that as a good sign, as proof he had hurt Cutler more than Cutler was willing to acknowledge. Darting to the right, he immediately reversed himself, shifted, and drove a fist into Pike Cutler's side again. A grimace was his reward. Before the man mountain could retaliate, he bounded to the rear.

Cutler lowered his arms a bit so his elbows protected his rib cage. "You're a sly one, I'll grant you that. But being devious is a poor substitute for sheer brawn. I can lift five hundred pounds over my head without hardly trying. Can you make the same claim?"

Fargo was tired of hearing the man crow about himself. "Talk is cheap. If you're so damn tough, prove it."

"Very well. I will."

Braced for a rush, Fargo balanced on the balls of his feet so he could skip to either side when Cutler came at him. But even though he was prepared for anything, or thought he was, the man mountain still took him off guard by surging toward him so fast he was nearly bowled over. He flung a fist but it had no more effect than a pea would on a boulder. A huge fist grazed his shoulder, jarring him, and as he dodged another swing, Cutler kicked him in the hip.

Catapulted across the grass, Fargo rolled to a stop close to the Chemehuevis. His left leg was numb, his pelvis in torment. As he rose he heard one of the Paiutes cry his name in warning. Hastina, he guessed as he spun to confront the man they both despised. Only Cutler was already there, right on top of him, looming like a runaway steam engine. Fargo hiked both arms to protect himself but he was too late. A fist nailed him in the gut.

Bursts of bright light blossomed before Fargo's eyes. He doubled over, his stomach churning, afraid he would retch. His lungs strained for breath, his legs grew wobbly. A hand locked onto his throat, another onto his waist. Thinking Cutler was about to strangle him, he swatted at the giant's arms. But Pike Cutler had a different idea.

"Let this be proof I do not make idle boasts."

Fargo struggled to break free but couldn't. The next moment his legs were swept out from under him as he was lifted bodily off the ground. The world turned upside down. He glimpsed the grass, glimpsed some of the Paiutes and gunmen, then saw Cutler staring up at him in vicious spite and realized that Cutler had raised him overhead, a feat few could do. He was shaken, as a terrier might shake a mouse, shaken so roughly his teeth ground together.

"See, Trailsman? I'm not even straining."

Fargo was. He strained to the right and the left, to the front and the back, wriggling like a slippery eel. He kicked at Cutler's head but could not quite reach him. He tried to jab Cutler in the eyes but Cutler merely laughed.

"Let's see if you'll bounce."

It took a second for Fargo to fathom what the giant meant, and in that fleeting interval he was hoisted higher. As he grabbed at Cutler's wrists, Cutler's arms swept forward. Air gushed past Fargo's face. He tried to land on his shoulder but he could not tell which way was up, let alone where he was in relation to the ground. Like a boulder falling from a great height he crashed onto the earth and was still, the breath knocked out of him, every joint molten fire, his whole body pulsing with agony.

Cutler placed his hands on his hips and turned to rake the circle with a critical gaze. "Do you see? The vaunted Trailsman is no more of a challenge than a child would be. Stick with me and before too long all of you will have more money than you'll know what to do with."

"How much exactly?" someone had the nerve to bluntly ask.

"A conservative estimate would be five thousand dollars," Cutler said.

"For all of us to share?"

"No, no. You misunderstood. *Each* of you will receive a full five thousand, if not a lot more. That's more money than most of you have ever held in your hands at one time. More than you will see in your lifetimes. So stick with me, gentlemen, and I guarantee you won't regret it."

Fargo slowly pushed onto his hands and knees. For the moment they had forgotten about him, including their leader. Focusing on the backs of Cutler's legs, he thrust a shoulder forward and hurtled at them in a blur, pumping his own legs like pistons.

"Boss! Look out!" someone cried.

The giant started to turn but Fargo was on him before he could. Fargo drove his shoulder between the tree trunks that served as Cutler's lower limbs, and for an excruciating moment so much pain exploded inside of him that it was almost as if he *had* tried to tackle trees. There was a crack so loud that Fargo half expected his collarbone had been shattered. He heard Pike Cutler grunt and pressure on his back as Cutler tumbled rearward.

Fargo scrambled forward another few yards, out from under his massive enemy. He pitched onto his chest, his left forearm caught underneath him. Pushing onto his knees, he shifted to ward off Cutler. But the human mountain was not poised to pounce.

Cutler was on his backside, mouth agape, astounded by the turn of events. "You knocked me off my feet," he declared in disbelief. "No one has ever done that before." Slowly rising, he rubbed the back of his right leg. "You're chock full of surprises, aren't you, Mr. Fargo? But then, I rated you as too much of a gentleman to attack me while my back was turned."

The man was too ridiculous for words. There were no rules in a fight to the death, and Fargo said as much as he stood.

"Suit yourself," Cutler said in annoyance. "Just remember that two can play at that game." So saying, he hurled himself across the grass with his own shoulders down low and his arms flung wide. To be caught in their unbreakable grip spelled certain death.

Fargo crouched, but did not move aside. Not yet. He waited until Cutler was almost on top of him, until the last possible instant, then he darted to the right. Cutler anticipated as much and slanted toward him. Fingers that could effortlessly bend spoons clutched at his shirt. Twisting, Fargo sprang to the left, into the clear, gaining a short respite.

Cutler pounded on by, then drew up short and pivoted. "You begin to annoy me, Trailsman," he said with keen resentment. "Few have ever given me so much trouble."

Fargo noticed that the giant was breathing heavily, much heavier than he should, since Cutler had not really exerted himself yet. In a flash of comprehension he saw the other's weakness, and he grinned. The man had no stamina.

"You find that amusing?" Cutler asked. "Astounding. You are a remarkable individual. Evidently your reputation is much more deserved than I presumed." He adopted a boxing posture again. "Well, shall we get this over with? You can only delay the inevitable for so long."

"We'll see about that," Fargo countered, sliding to the left. Cutler rotated as he did, those macelike fists cocked to bash his brains out if he came within range. Suddenly Fargo did just that. He bounded forward, and predictably Cutler swung a right cross that would have felled him like a poled ox had it landed. But as Pike Cutler leaned into the punch, Fargo darted on around him and drove his own right fist into the bigger man's kidney, then backpedaled before Cutler could retaliate.

The would-be emperor turned. His face was an ugly mask of savage hatred. "I'm going to grind your bones to dust with my bare hands and stomp on your head until it splits like a melon."

The man talked too much. In his supreme self-confidence, Cutler made one of the most basic of mistakes. In a fight, a person should *fight*, not blabber on like biddies at a quilting social. Pausing to spout threats gave an adversary time to catch his breath and plot strategy. "If this was a battle of words, you'd win hands down," Fargo said.

"You'd rather I shut up and attend to the business at hand? So be it," Pike Cutler declared, and attacked in earnest.

It was like trying to ward off a tornado. Fargo brought up his arms to defend himself but they were buffeted by blows so powerful that each jolted him backward. He tried to skip to the right but this time Cutler stayed glued to him like a shadow. He danced to the left with the same result. And with every step Cutler took, his enormous arms pumped in steady cadence.

Wham-wham-wham. The punches rained onto Fargo, fast and furious. He was battered, buffeted, pummeled. Granite knuckles grazed his temple, dazing him. His ribs nearly buckled. He took another hit to the stomach and the world spun madly. The fists he threw were blocked, battered aside as if they were the feeble blows of a day-old infant. The onslaught drove him backward, ever backward, until he bumped into someone and was roughly shoved. It drove him forward, into Cutler, who slammed a crushing left into his side.

A keg of black powder went off inside. Fargo crumbled to his knees, scarcely able to breathe or think. He glanced up at Pike Cutler, who sneered down in wicked triumph and nudged him with a toe.

"What's the matter, Trailsman? No more insults? Any last *words* you'd like to say?"

Gruff laughter greeted the ridicule. Fargo saw that they were close to the ring of gunmen. Beyond lay comforting darkness, and salvation. But he would be shot dead if he were to make a break for it. Unless he had some unwitting help. Marshaling his strength, he slowly straightened and raised his fists once more. "This isn't over yet," he said. "And if you can't hit any harder than you have been, I don't have anything to worry about."

Pike Cutler flushed scarlet. Drawing back his right arm, he put all of his weight into his next blow. It would kill Fargo if it landed. But by telegraphing it, Cutler inadvertently played right into Fargo's hands.

As the malletlike fist swept toward him, Fargo flung himself backward. His timing had to be perfect if he was to trick the gunmen. He must not make it appear that he wanted to be knocked halfway to Sunday. It must seem that Cutler clipped him just hard enough for his purpose.

The punch caught him on the jaw a fraction of an instant sooner than Fargo would have liked, but the result was the same. He was propelled into the ring of badmen, into them and past them as they sprang aside so they would not be bowled over. Tottering wildly, he fell. More laughter pealed, and one of the hardcases shouted, "Look at him! He ain't so high and mighty now, is he?"

They were having so much fun at his expense, none of them showed much concern that he was now outside the circle and lying at the edge of the area bathed by lantern light. Fargo rose unsteadily onto his elbows and shook his groggy head to clear it.

"Haul him back, boys," Cutler commanded. "Let's finish this farce so you can get on with your drinking."

A couple of gunmen moved to obey. Fargo had delayed too long. But he would never, ever give up without a struggle. Flipping onto his side, he heaved upright and bolted into the night, his shaky legs threatening to spoil everything.

Yells and curses erupted. Several shots were snapped but missed. "Quit firing!" Pike Cutler roared. "I want him alive, damn it! A hundred dollars to the man who catches our famous guest!"

Boots drummed in a stampede of eager cutthroats. Fargo risked a glance and saw them spreading out to prevent him from going to the north or the south. Let them. He had something else in mind. Willing his legs to cooperate, he sprinted to the east, toward the river. He had an eight-yard lead but that had dropped to six when the silhouette of the bank hove into sight. Without slowing, Fargo made for the edge, sucked in all the air he could into his lungs, and launched himself into a shallow dive. If his memory served, at that point there was a pool. Not a deep one, but deep enough.

Chilly, clammy water closed around his body, clearing his head in a rush. Fargo brushed the bottom and leveled off. Turning to the south, he swam with smooth, practiced strokes. Muted voices above warned that if he broke the surface too soon, he would be spotted. He continued to swim until the voices were to his rear, until his lungs were fit to rupture if he did not take a breath. Then he angled upward. He thought he had gone far enough. He figured he would be safe. But he was wrong.

There was a commotion on the bank and a hard case hollered, "Here he is! He's a-goin' this-a-way!" Someone leaped into the river and splashed toward him.

Taking another breath, Fargo bent at the waist and dived. He kept on swimming, hugging the bottom. His lungs started to hurt but he suppressed the pain. He must go farther than the last time, farther than he had ever gone underwater before, farther than the gun sharks would think was humanly possible. His arms and legs cleaving the water in a smooth rhythm, he swam and swam and swam. Only when the agony in his chest was unbearable and he was on the verge of passing out did he angle upward again.

No shouts rang out. Twenty yards to the north scurrying shapes flitted along the river's edge. Others were in the water, making more noise than bathing buffalo. He dived for a third time and continued on. When next he poked his head up, the racket and the figures were far behind. He had done it! He was safe!

Elated but weary, Fargo moved to the shore and trudged up an incline. The woods were nearby. He would hide out until daylight and plan his next move. Taking a tired step, he raised a hand to his throbbing head and discovered his hat was gone. It was then that a human form reared up out of the darkness and sprang.

11

Skye Fargo could not leap out of the way or bring a hand up quickly enough to defend himself. The apparition was on him in a lithe bound. Slender arms enfolded his chest. Hot lips pressed against his neck and lavished hungry kisses on his throat and chin. Bewildered, he gripped the figure's shapely shoulders. "Winnemucca?"

"It is I," the maiden said lustily, and locked her mouth to his.

Any other time or place Fargo would have been flattered by her ardor. But at the moment they had a pressing problem to deal with, as outcries and faint furtive movement reminded him. Peeling the Chemehuevi off, he whispered into her ear, "We need to find a place to hide."

Winnemucca clasped his hand. "Come with me," She said, and led him back into the river.

Fargo would rather have gone into the forest but he trusted her judgment. They swiftly crossed without hindrance. Bent low, they scooted into the trees and hastened eastward, the maiden threading through the undergrowth with the ease and speed of a doe. Questions were on the tip of his tongue but he held off asking them. The din at the river faded. Presently they neared the towering eastern ramparts, the red cliffs that gave Red Valley its name. Winnemucca slowed and scoured the woods as if searching for a landmark. When they came to a lightning-blasted bole, she smiled and bent her steps to the southwest.

The vegetation soon ended. Above them reared the inky cliffs, so high they seemed to touch the sky. The maiden moved to the base and hurried southward. In a couple of hundred feet she tugged at his arm and pointed at a black cavity.

It was a small cave, eight feet wide and six feet high at the entrance. Just inside stones had been piled waist-high from the left-hand side almost to the right, leaving a narrow gap. Winnemucca stepped on around. Fargo paused to let his eyes become accustomed to the gloom. He heard the maiden move about. The crack of a fire steel on flint produced a spark that briefly lit her face and hunched form. She was bent over a pile of kindling. Another try, and the kindling caught. Expertly, Winnemucca leaned down and puffed on the tiny flame. It grew rapidly. She added small branches from a stack set against the wall, just enough to make a small fire.

"There. We can see."

The cave extended back a dozen feet. Folded blankets and several baskets told Fargo it saw regular use. "What is this place?" he inquired as he sat beside her.

Winnemucca grinned coyly. "My people come here sometimes. Men and women, to be alone."

She did not go into detail, but she did not have to. It was a hideaway for lovers, a place couples came so they would not be disturbed. On the walls were crude paintings of men and animals, done with reddish pigment. The men carried bows and spears and clubs. Some of the animals Fargo recognized; bison, deer, and bears. But there were other creatures new to him, one with a hump on its back and a long trunk and tusks that looked for all the world like an elephant from darkest Africa. Another was a huge bearlike creature with a long, thick tail that stood on two legs eating leaves. Yet another was a monster cat with two fangs that hung past its chin. Ancient paintings, Fargo judged, done long before white men set foot on North America.

"Cutler has not learned of this place, and others," Winnemucca said. "My people know every nook and cranny of Red Valley. We should. It has been ours since the beginning of all things."

"What are you doing here? How did you happen to find me?"

"When I woke up in the village and found you had gone, I took the mare and followed you. I did not come in the north end of the valley, as you did, because I know Cutler keeps men on guard there." Winnemucca leaned closer, the firelight playing over her lovely face and sparkling eyes. "I came in by a way known only to the Chemehuevis. I hid the mare, then snuck close to the house."

Fargo was impressed by her courage. "You've been spying on them the whole time?"

She nodded. "Waiting for a chance to help you. I saw you ride off yesterday but there were too many of Cutler's men around for me to show myself. Tonight, I watched the fight. When you ran and jumped in the river, I was going to come to you but Cutler's men were everywhere. In order not to be caught, I had to move farther and farther away. Then I heard a noise in the water, and you appeared."

Fargo was grateful she had shown up when she did, but now she was in deadly danger. Should she be caught at his side, Cutler would not hesitate to put her to death. "You should have stayed with your people where it was safe."

Winnemucca pouted. "You are not glad to see me? After all I have gone through?"

"I never said that," Fargo responded. "Fact is, I'm happy you're here. But I don't want you harmed—" He got no further. She squealed for joy and threw her arms around him again, her lips molding to his in a display of fiery emotion.

Fargo was sore all over and weary as could be. He was battered and bruised. His body had more welts and bumps and scrapes than he cared to count. By rights, he should lie right down and get some rest. But when Winnemucca kissed him, his aches and woes evaporated like dew under the morning sun. He was *alive*, and that was all that counted. Sliding his tongue into her velvety mouth, he swirled it around. Her tongue entwined with his, and her indescribably sweet taste was enough to stir his groin.

"I am glad you are alive," the maiden commented when they parted. Her finger traced along the outer edge of his right ear and down over his neck.

"That makes two of us." Fargo leaned against the stone wall and relaxed for the first time since he had been caught by Rufus and Lafferty. As the tension drained out of him like water from a sieve, pain took its place. His arms pulsed with torment, his stomach was a cauldron of discomfort. When Winnemucca sidled over and placed a hand on his chest, he could not help flinching.

"Oh. You are badly hurt."

"Let's just say that I won't be breaking mustangs for a spell." Fargo touched a nasty bump on his temple. When he moved, his ribs were racked by a short spasm. He hoped to high heaven none of them were broken because it would not do to be laid up. Not as anxious as he was to settle accounts with Pike Cutler.

Winnemucca nuzzled close without actually touching him. "You need to sleep awhile. When you wake up, I will have good news for you."

"What news?"

Smiling, the maiden brushed his lips with hers. "I would rather keep it a secret until later. For now, we must make you comfortable." Standing, she collected the blankets and spread them out to the rear of the fire, then opened one of the baskets. "Are you hungry?"

"I could eat a buffalo raw," Fargo admitted. He had no inclination to budge, but since she had gone to so much bother he stiffly rose and settled onto their makeshift bed.

Winnemucca slid the basket toward him. "There is not much left, but what there is, you can have."

It contained five pieces of jerked venison. Old jerky, to judge by how dry the pieces were, but to Fargo they tasted as delicious as fresh roasted steaks. He offered one to Winnemucca but she declined. Polishing off three, he gave her the basket and lay down, his head cradled on his arm. He had a lot to ponder. For starters, how to turn the tables on the outlaws when he was hopelessly outnumbered and unarmed.

The warmth of the fire and the coziness of the cave lulled Fargo into feeling drowsy. He did not mean to, but he fell asleep and slept the sleep of the dead, oblivious to the world. When he opened his eyes it was the middle of the night. The fire had burned out. His gut felt lots better and his arms were not half as bad as they had been. Shifting to make himself comfortable, he bumped into the still form of Winnemucca. She had stretched out beside him, so close that he felt her breath on his cheek when he eased onto his shoulder, facing her. Taking it for granted she was asleep, Fargo gently draped an arm over her and closed his eyes. Another couple of hour's rest and he would be as fit as the proverbial fiddle.

"You are awake?"

"You, too?" Fargo rejoined. "Sorry if I woke you."

Winnemucca slid nearer, her nose so close that he could have flicked his tongue and licked the tip. "I have missed you. What we did in the lodge was very special to me." She paused, and Fargo feared she was about to say that they made a perfect couple and should spend the rest of their lives together. But she surprised him. "I know you will leave when your work here is done. I know no woman will ever have a hold over you. But that is not important to me. This is."

Fargo's mouth received hers. She pressed forward, her hands running through his hair as her ripe body molded to his. He only intended to kiss her and go back to sleep. But then one of her hands lowered to the junction of his legs and brazenly cupped his hardening organ. Her audacity shocked and delighted him. "What exactly do you have in mind?" he asked playfully.

Winnemucca bowed her head. "I like you, Skye Fargo. You made me tingle inside. I would like to tingle again before you go. As many times as you want."

Something came over him. Whether it was her innocent appeal, her girlish shyness, or the warmth of her hand on his manhood, Fargo could not say. Maybe it was a combination of all three. Suddenly he wanted her as much as she wanted him, and his bruises be damned. His mouth found hers, soft and wanting, and his hand climbed her hip to the flat of her belly. She cooed and squirmed in sensual anticipation.

Fargo roved his hand higher, to her glorious globes. Winnemucca gasped when he squeezed one, her nipple growing rigid. The same with her other breast when he switched to it. She ground her hips against him, her mouth greedily devouring his, her hands trying to be everywhere at once. Her whole body was as hot as a stove. Plainly, she had not exaggerated her carnal craving.

Hiking her dress, Fargo slid his hand underneath. Her skin was satiny to the touch, goose bumps erupting under his fingertips as he massaged a path up her right leg to her silken inner thigh. She threw back her head and sighed in contentment. Kneading her exquisitely soft flesh, he edged higher by gradual degrees, prolonging the thrill of first contact with her simmering core.

Winnemucca cried out softly when Fargo's palm brushed across her bush. He pressed lightly and rubbed in a clockwise motion, eliciting a groan amplified by the confines of the cave. Her thighs automatically parted wide. He dallied, lowering his middle finger to rub her tiny knob. Wheezing lustily, Winnemucca thrust against him.

"I want you so much."

Fargo could tell. He stroked her nether lips to the rim of her soaked tunnel, prompting her to fling her lower legs around his back and clamp hold as if afraid he would get up and leave. Dipping a finger into her womanhood, Fargo held it still while she shook and quivered in physical rapture. Her tongue was doing wondrous things to his ear, while her hand was doing its best to stoke his desire to a red-hot peak.

Lowering her onto her back, Fargo started to pull the dress higher. She obliged him by raising it herself. Her breasts spilled out, enticing, alluring. Seeking a nipple, he lathered it while his hand began to stroke her slit. Whining, Winnemucca closed her legs on his arm. "Oh! Oh!" she exclaimed, already on the brink.

Fargo gave her mounds the attention they deserved. The longer he kissed and licked, the more they seemed to expand. She licked her lips and moaned and rolled her head as if delirious. The time was ripe. Stiffening his middle finger,

Fargo plunged it into her. Winnemucca shot up off the blankets, clawing at him, her teeth sinking into his shoulder.

Raw lust coursed through Fargo's veins. He sucked a nipple into his mouth and rolled it with his tongue. All the while his finger plunged in and out, in and out, his thumb brushing her knob with every stroke. She opened her mouth in a soundless scream, her eyes flared, reaching her climax long before he was ready. Heaving upward, she thrust against him repeatedly, lost in the pure ecstasy of a shattering release.

Fargo stopped stroking and she gradually calmed, coasting to a stop. Her breaths came in raspy bursts and her eyelids flittered. He nibbled on her ear, provoking a giggle.

"I tingled again."

"It won't be the last time," Fargo promised, applying his lips to the base of her throat. She wriggled seductively as he massaged her skin with his mouth. Cupping both taut breasts, he created enough friction to ignite another fire by rubbing them until they were coals. Her legs parted again, the dank scent of her femaleness filling the cave. His mouth watered, but not for food.

"Do I make you feel as good as you make me feel?" Winnemucca asked.

Fargo was too preoccupied to answer. She was making the same mistake Cutler had made; talking too much. To silence her he welded his mouth to hers and let their tongues join in mutual caress. Her hips began to pump again, slowly at first, but with more urgency when his left hand dropped to her bushy knoll and his finger caressed her crack.

Winnemucca raked his back, his arms. The former he did not mind. The latter aggravated his bruises and welts, intruding pain into his pleasure. But short of slapping her hands, he had to endure it and blot the pangs from his mind.

Fargo reached down to undo his pants but she'd had the notion first. Her fingers tugged at his belt, then at his britches, fumbling awkwardly to push them down. Her inexperience was as glaring as her sexual hunger. Once his pole popped free, she grasped it at the stem and roughly ran her hands up and down. Too roughly. He had to grip her wrist and show her how to do it properly. Once she understood, she delicately caressed him for minutes on end, blissfully unaware of the effect she was having. A constriction formed in Fargo's throat, and a sensation akin to a lit fuse burned deep in his organ. A fuse that sizzled shorter and shorter the longer her fingers plied his rigid member.

Fargo was close to exploding when he yanked her hands off and buried himself inside of her in one fell swoop, plunging to the limit in a driving thrust that half lifted her off the ground. "Ohhhhhh!" she cried, grasping his shoulders. Her legs enclosed his back, her mouth parted invitingly. In that instant of erotic abandon she was the living embodiment of every man's fantasy.

"Again!" Winnemucca exclaimed in wonder. "I'm doing it again!"

Levering his knees forward, Fargo commenced pumping, going faster and faster and faster. She matched him, stroke for stroke. When they were rocking as fast as they could possibly go, she stifled a scream by biting her own forearm. It was the trigger for his own release, an internal blast that roiled up within him and eclipsed all conscious thought. His senses soared to a pinnacle higher than Mount Dutton. For long seconds he had the impression that he was adrift high in the sky, floating like a cloud, every nerve vibrant.

Then the moment passed and Fargo settled down to earth. He was lying on top of Winnemucca, the two of them totally spent. Her limbs were askew, her limpid eyes gazing fondly into his.

"Thank you."

Fargo pecked her cheek and rolled onto his side, too tired to pull his pants back up. He closed his eyes and was immediately asleep. Not meaning to, he slept until a pale streak pierced the dawn sky. Crisp air on his backside awakened him. Shivering slightly, he adjusted his pants and slowly rose. The rest had done him some good in that he felt greatly refreshed. But his arms were leaden and his ribs bit into him whenever he raised his arms higher than his waist.

Gingerly stretching, Fargo strode through the gap to the cave entrance. Deep shadow shrouded the strip of barren earth between the cliff and the forest. He gazed toward the trees, and was startled when over a dozen ghostly figures reared up close in front of him as if they had sprouted from the very earth. In pure reflex his hand stabbed for his missing pistol. It was probably just as well he did not have it or he might have squeezed off a shot before he saw that the specters were not Pike Cutler's men.

They were Chemehuevis.

Fargo recognized the old men from the village. They carried war clubs, knives, and lances, and stood in silence as if awaiting instructions. He started to back into the cave and bumped into Winnemucca, who had just emerged. "What is this?" he asked. "What are they doing here?"

"A council was held and they decided to do as you wanted. They are willing to fight." She squeezed his wrist and beamed. "This is the surprise I had. My people will not be used as slaves any longer. We will drive Cutler and his killers from our land so all whites will know that they cannot take what rightfully belongs to the Chemehuevis."

Fargo was dumbfounded. He had about given up on them. But now that they were ready to go to war, he had another problem. How was he to go about ending Cutler's reign of terror without getting all of the Paiutes killed?

As if Winnemucca were privy to his thoughts, she commented, "You need not worry whether we can fight or not. I know many whites think we are cowards. But they mistake a love of peace for a fear of death. Once the Chemehuevis make up their minds that blood must be spilled, we spill it as well as any other tribe."

"Our best bet is to wait until dark and hit Cutler's outfit while most of them are asleep in their bunks," Fargo plotted aloud. "Around two in the morning would be perfect. We'll set fire to the bunkhouse and pick them off as they come running out."

Winnemucca gave a strange little cough. "I am sorry. But we can not."

"Why?"

"My people do not wage war after the sun has set."

Fargo glanced at her, hoping she was joking. But she was in earnest. He didn't hold it against the Chemehuevis since some other tribes he knew of shared the belief. The Piegans, for instance, the most notorious white-haters west of the Mississippi, would never attack at night. The same with the Apaches, whose warriors were as fearless as any who ever lived but who were deathly afraid that if they died at night their spirits would not find their way to the Apache afterlife. Or something to that effect. "All right. We'll hit them this morning, fast and hard, while they least expect it."

Again Winnemucca coughed. "We can not do it just yet."

"Why not?"

She nodded at the elders. "Our warriors must go through a special ceremony. They have to purify themselves and see to their weapons."

Again Fargo understood. Other tribes performed similar rituals prior to going on raids. The Minniconjou Sioux smoked a war pipe and painted their war horses and spent the night before singing and dancing. The Shoshones did pretty much the same. Blackfeet warriors took part in sham battles. "Fair enough. We'll begin this afternoon."

The maiden scrunched up her face as if she had sucked on a lemon. "I am so sorry," she apologized once more, "but the ceremony will take most of the day."

"I give up. When the hell can we attack?"

"Tomorrow morning would be nice," Winnemucca said sweetly.

Fargo surveyed the half circle of elders, men long since past their prime, warriors who had not lifted a finger against another human being in years, probably decades. It was commendable they had a will to fight, but that alone was no substitute for *skill*. Cutler's men were born killers, one and all, men who lived by the gun and the blade, men who were highly proficient at what they did or they would not be alive. He had second thoughts about leading the

133

Chemehuevis against them. It would be like leading sheep against wolves.

"You can rest," Winnemucca suggested. "We will bring food and water. And I will find herbs for your wounds. By tomorrow you will feel fine."

Fargo had his doubts, but since he couldn't go up against Cutler's bunch alone, he had no choice but to twiddle his thumbs until the Chemehuevis were done with their preparations. "Wake me at noon if I'm not up by then," he said, turning into the cave.

"You sound upset? Are you mad at us?"

"Why would I be mad?" Fargo grumbled. "Just get it over with before winter sets in and I'll be a happy man." He did not mean to snap at her but he could not help being a trifle miffed. Why hadn't the Chemehuevis performed their ceremony *before* they showed up? Covering himself with a blanket, Fargo tossed and turned awhile, listening to chants outside. Finally he dozed off, not awakening until the sun was almost directly overhead.

Yawning and wiping the sleep from his eyes, Fargo stepped past the wall. It was unnaturally quiet, and he could not help wondering if the Chemehuevis had changed their minds and gone back to their village. But no, they were there, seated in pairs, one of each couple applying war paint to the other. The lanky warrior who knew a smattering of English smiled at him and declared, "We make big war. Bad whites all die."

"I admire a man with confidence," Fargo said dryly. He saw no sign of Winnemucca and was about to go to the river for a drink when she bounded out of the verdant growth and across the open space, bearing plants and a bulging water skin. "Where did you get that?" he asked.

"Monuso brought it," she said, pointing at the lanky man. "Come. I will tend you."

Fargo let her lead him inside again and stripped off his shirt at her bidding. In the light of day the welts and bruises and gashes were ghastly to behold. Winnemucca spent half an hour heating water and preparing a mix of herbs she made into a soothing salve. She applied some to every wound. It did not sting but the odor left a little to be desired. When she was done, Fargo felt as if he had been smeared with molasses. After a while the salve dried, though, and it was not so bad.

His stomach growled loud enough for both of them to hear. Winnemucca excused herself and was gone only a few minutes. When she came back, she said for him to wait and soon he would have plenty to eat. True to her word, before too long a warrior appeared with a freshly killed rabbit. "why do I get the idea you're waiting on me hand and foot?"

"Can we do less? You are risking your life for us." She tenderly caressed him with one hand while holding the bloody rabbit in the other. "No white man has ever done as you have done. Our people will always be grateful."

"Save your thanks. If something goes wrong Cutler is liable to wipe out your whole tribe and it will be my fault for stirring your people up against him."

"We will win. We are in the right."

Fargo frowned. Naive attitudes like that got a lot of people killed. Being in the right gave no guarantees. Any past war proved as much. Both sides usually thought God favored them over their enemy, yet one side always lost. In this case the lines were more clearly drawn. Pike Cutler was a vicious bastard who deserved to be turned into worm food, but Cutler still might come out on top. The way Fargo saw it, in war it wasn't a simple matter of who was right and who was wrong. Being bloodthirsty counted for more than being moral, and in that respect Cutler's cutthroats had an edge.

The afternoon was uneventful. Hour after hour the warriors sang and chanted and danced. Each bore symbols on his face, chest, arms, or legs. As evening fell they sat in a large circle and each Paiute quietly sang a different song to himself.

"It is their death song," Winnemucca explained. "In case they do not live through tomorrow."

The Chemehuevis had not eaten a bite all day. Fargo suggested hunting game enough for all but the maiden shook her head.

"They will not take food until after the battle. It is our custom."

"Any others I should know about?" Fargo absently asked, more out of irritation than interest. The Chemehuevis were sticklers for doing everything just so to avoid bad medicine, and he did not want to do anything they would construe as a bad omen.

Winnemucca reflected a bit, then nodded. "Just one. Maybe I should have mentioned it sooner. It might have a bearing on how you fight Cutler." She paused. "If a Chemehuevi warrior is slain, the rest will stop fighting and carry him away to be buried."

All Fargo could do was stare at her.

12

An hour after sunrise eight young Paiute warriors plodded along the rutted trail that wound through the middle of Red Valley. They trailed a rattling wagon, the driver cracking his whip over the heads of the team again and again. In the wagon bed sat a grungy man holding a shotgun. To the rear rode two more guards armed with rifles.

Presently the column came to a clearing where timber had been felled the day before. The two guards dismounted and took up posts on either side. The man with the scatter-gun stayed where he was, chewing on a wad of tobacco. It was the driver who passed out axes and other tools to the weary Chemehuevis and directed them toward certain trees.

"Remember, you heathens," he said, "Pike wants four whole loads today or you don't get any supper tonight. Just like last night."

The shotgun guard snickered. "Cutler sure has been on a tear since that feller gave us the slip. Did you hear the tongue-lashing he gave poor Lucius? Why, I thought he was going to break Quay in two after all we found was that jasper's hat."

Hidden in the thick growth that rimmed the clearing, Skye Fargo overheard and smiled. Any aggravation he caused Pike Cutler was well worth it. He glanced to the right and the left at the waiting line of Chemehuevis, then at Winnemucca, who was crouched beside him. It had not been his idea to bring her. He would much rather have the maiden safe and secure in the cave. But she had argued heatedly, making the point that of all her tribe she was best able to translate his commands. Her grasp of English was far superior to that of Monuso or any other. Reluctantly, Fargo had given in. He had to. Whether they won or were slaughtered might well depend on having his directions carried out to the letter.

Now Fargo gestured, and Winnemucca in turn motioned to either side. He had rehearsed the warriors in the part they were to play, an supposedly they had their parts down pat. If not, the campaign to reclaim Red Valley was doomed before it really started.

The older warriors melted into the vegetation, except for four who were to stay by Fargo at all times. Not so much as a leaf rustled. He had to admit the Chemehuevis were more skilled than he had given them credit for being.

One of the young Paiutes was coming toward a tree near the patch of high weeds that hid Fargo and his companions. It was Hastina. Fargo checked that none of the guards were gazing in his direction, then pushed up high enough for the muscular Chemehuevi to see him and immediately flattened again.

Hastina never broke stride. He blinked once, and that was it. The ax over his shoulder, he stopped next to the trunk.

"Don't dawdle, you mangy redskins," the driver hollered. "Get to swinging or I'll let you have a taste of my whip's lash."

The thunk of steel biting into bark resounded as the captives obeyed. In the wagon the shotgun guard pulled a plug of tobacco from a shirt pocket and bit off another chaw. The driver climbed onto the seat and treated himself to a sip from a small flask he had under his vest. One of the riflemen leaned against a willow. The other hunkered and doodled in the dirt with a stick. Apparently they did not regard the Chemehuevis as much of a threat.

Which was fine by Fargo. He watched the wall of vegetation across the clearing, and at length a bronzed silhouette briefly appeared. The older warriors were in position. But he did not give the order to attack just yet. They had to be extremely careful not to let any of the gunmen snap off a shot. The breeze could carry the sound a long way and possibly alert others.

Hastina was swinging his ax with zeal. Every now and again he glanced at the weeds and grinned like a kid who had just been given a handful of hard candy.

A bee buzzed past Fargo's face but he paid it no mind. Butterflies flitted among flowers at the clearing's edge. Robins and sparrows chirped gaily deeper in the woods. The peaceful setting was bound to have an effect on the four bored, tired guards. Soon enough, it did. The rifleman who had leaned against the willow closed his eyes, dozing. The driver took to yawning and shaking himself to stay awake. Only the shotgun guard was fully alert, his head swiveling every which way.

Winnemucca nudged Fargo and arched her eyebrows but he shook his head. Patience was called for. No matter how long it took, he was not giving the word until the time was right. Half an hour went by. An hour. The maiden fidgeted but not the four older warriors. They lay perfectly still, wrinkled statues impervious to the heat and the insects. So was Fargo.

Then the shotgun guard rose and clambered over the side of the wagon. "Nature calls," the man said. "Be right back."

"Don't dribble on yourself," the driver joked.

The guard spat some tobacco, grinned, and ambled toward brush to the north of the clearing. He picked a spot between two of the young warriors, halted, and fiddled with the front of his pants. The shotgun was cradled in his left elbow.

Fargo turned to Winnemucca. *"Now!"*

She relayed the command to an elder on her left, who instantly drew back the sinew string to his short ash bow, rose onto his knees, and sent the arrow straight up into the sky. Fargo hoped that none of the gunmen would notice but as luck would have it the driver did. Gawking, the man blurted, "What the hell?" They were the last words he would ever utter.

The shotgun guard suddenly stumbled backward, dropping the scattergun as he gripped the heavy shaft of a lance that jutted from his chest. Pivoting, he extended an arm in mute appeal, then keeled over, dead on his feet. As he fell, the two riflemen straightened in alarm and swung toward him. They rushed to his aid but neither took more than a couple of strides when they were transfixed from behind, one by a lance, the other by two glittering shafts. The first man toppled but the second spun, snarling like a beast at bay, and began to level his rifle. Just as his finger was curling around the trigger a third arrow whizzed out of the greenery and sliced into the base of his throat. The man fell, gurgling and sputtering.

That left the driver. It had all happened so fast, he had not had time to resort to his revolver. As the last of his friends fell, he scooped up the reins and whip and frantically lashed the team, seeking to get out of there before he shared their fate.

The wizened warrior who had given the initial signal burst from cover, sighted along another arrow, and let fly. Like a wooden bolt of lightning it flew true to the mark, the barked tip coring the driver's left eye and catapulting him off the wagon in a whirl of limbs. The man hit hard and did not stir.

Just like that, it was over.

Fargo moved into the open. On cue, the older warriors did the same and were greeted warmly by Hastina and the rest of the younger men. "Tell them they can celebrate later," he directed Winnemucca. "Right now we have to get rid of the bodies and hide the wagon before more of Cutler's boys come along."

He had to handle the wagon himself. After the bodies were dumped in the bed, he wheeled it into the forest far enough back that riders passing by on the trail would not be apt to notice.

As a result of their first victory they now had six revolvers, two rifles, and a shotgun. Plus ammunition. Fargo selected a short-barreled Colt with fine balance and nickel plating. He also kept a rifle. The others he gave to Winnemucca, saying, "Pass them out to whoever wants one." She gave the word to the men, but to Fargo's surprise none of the warriors stepped forward. "What's wrong? Don't they like using guns?"

Winnemucca broached the question. Hastina answered for all of them, and she relayed what he had said. "It is not that they don't like using guns. It is just that they do not know how. None of them has ever owned a rifle or fired a pistol. They do not think they would be able to hit anything."

Fargo swore under his breath. He should have thought of that himself. Shoving the shotgun at Winnemucca, he dashed to the weeds to stash the rest of the hardware. She dogged his footsteps.

"What am I to do with this? I have never fired a gun, either."

"Keep it for later, just in case." Fargo showed her how to thumb back the twin hammers and demonstrated how to hold the stock tucked to her side so the recoil wouldn't kick her backward or tear the weapon from her hands.

The Chemehuevis gathered around, awaiting instructions. They were smiling and happy, their spirits bolstered by their success. But Fargo knew they were as changeable as the weather. Should one of them die, he would be on his own. It handicapped him, limiting the strategy he could adopt. Whatever course he chose must be as safe for the Chemehuevis as was humanly possible.

But Fargo wasn't fooling himself. The chances of making it through the day without casualties were slim to none. Should it happen sooner rather than later, eliminating Cutler would be much more difficult.

Hastina spoke to Winnemucca, who translated. "Hastina says to thank you for freeing him and the others. He says that he sensed you were a friend the first time he saw you." She paused to listen. "He says that they were beaten and whipped every day. That they were given little food and water. That they were shackled at night. Helpless, they would listen to their women cry and groan. And they grew mad inside. Mad like they have never been mad before. So mad that he and the other young warriors will not rest until Pike Cutler and every last one of his killers are all dead."

Fargo nodded at the strapping warrior. Their zeal was commendable, but their hankering for vengeance might make them careless. Yet another concern he must keep in mind. "Tell the young ones the same thing you told the old men," he directed. "They are to do exactly as I say at all times. No one—and I mean *no one*—is to make a move against Cutler's men unless I give the word. Do they understand?"

After all the younger Paiutes replied that they did, Fargo started across the clearing. A nicker reminded him of the two mounts belonging to the riflemen. Both horses had been tied to a small tree when the work party arrived. But now only one of the animals was there. "What happened to the other one?" he asked Winnemucca.

The maiden relayed the question and an elder answered. "It ran off during the fight."

Alarm spiked through Fargo. "Ran off where?"

"Back down the trail."

"Damn." Breaking into a run, Fargo jogged southward, the Chemehuevis keeping pace behind him. The horse was nowhere to be seen, and he could well imagine what would happen when it showed up at the stable minus its owner. Cutler would be suspicious, and on the alert. Gunmen would be sent to investigate. Either that, or Cutler would lead them himself.

Fargo ran faster. How much time they had depended on whether the horse trotted straight to the stable or stopped along the way. He stuck to the edge of the wide trail so he could dart into the vegetation at a moment's notice and ordered Winnemucca to have the Paiutes follow his example.

It was half a mile to the edge of the woodland. Fargo did not slacken his pace once, yet he was not breathing hard when they arrived. Nor were the Chemehuevis. Living in the wild had made them whipcord tough, as it would anyone. Not as tough as Apaches, say, who could cover seventy-five miles at a stretch afoot and be no worse for wear. But they were hardy enough to travel incredibly long distances without tiring.

Hunkering in the shadow of a cottonwood, Fargo scanned

the tilled fields. As usual, captive females were engaged in a variety of tasks under the watchful eyes of several guards. He counted eleven women, all told. Some were pulling weeds, others hoeing, some raking, some digging.

Fargo was more interested in the hardcases. Two patrolled the fields, walking up and down the rows. The third man was close to the trail. Seated with is back to it, he had his hat brim pulled low over his face and was evidently dozing. Fargo wondered why none of the three had noticed the riderless horse go by, as it surely must have unless it had strayed off to the west to graze.

A lean Chemehuevi near him stirred and growled like a wild beast. Fargo looked, and saw that one of the guards had stopped beside a shapely Paiute woman and was lecherously fondling her posterior. Rigid with fear, the woman did not resist.

"It is Kachemic's wife," Winnemucca whispered.

Fargo lunged just as the Chemehuevi began to rise, gripping the furious husband's wrist. "Tell him to wait. Tell him I share his anger, but rushing out there will only get him killed and spoil everything."

Urgently, Winnemucca passed it on. The young warrior's jaw muscles twitched and he clenched his fists until his knuckles were pale, but he did not give rein to his wrath. Sinking onto a knee, he bowed his head and trembled in stoic outrage.

Fargo let go. Pointing at Hastina and four of the older men, he motioned for them to form a small circle around him. The furious husband looked up, and against Fargo's better judgment he signed for the man to join them. Winnemucca interpreted.

"Three of you will go after each of the whites in the field. I will take care of the man by the trail. Use knives. Take them unawares and slit their throats. Above all else, you must not let them cry out or fire a shot. Any questions?"

"How will we know when to strike?" Hastina asked.

"Watch this spot. When I nod to Winnemucca, she will wave her arm. That will be the signal."

Like a pride of panthers slinking off to stalk antelope, the Chemehuevis crept in among the stalks of corn, and were gone. Fargo borrowed a knife from Monuso, then bent close to the maiden. "Don't let any of the others get any fool notions. Remind them there are still captives at the house, and Cutler isn't above butchering them out of spite."

"Do not worry. None of us will do anything to put our brothers and sisters at risk."

Nodding, Fargo dropped into a crouch and dashed in among the stalks. They were chest-high, spaced close together in row after glistening green row, their ranks broken by narrow irrigation ditches at thirty-foot intervals. The soil was soft, in contrast to the baked iron hardness of the blistered wasteland that surrounded Red Valley. He made no more noise than the breeze as he closed on his quarry.

It took ten minutes to get into position. Fargo had to stay low to avoid rustling the stalks. He had forty feet to go when a slender girl in her teens spotted him. She was bent over, plucking weeds, and happened to glance around as he glided between rows. Her eyes widened but she did not give him away. Smiling, he poked a finger at the sleeping guard, then drew the knife across his neck in imitation of what he intended to do. The girl showed more teeth than a patent medicine salesman trying to sell a cure-all elixir.

Fargo snuck on, parting the broad blades of the tall plants with a forearm, careful not to let the sharp edges cut his hands or face. He was maybe twenty feet from the gunman when an unforeseen element intruded itself.

Hooves drummed to the north. Riders were approaching. The dozing guard sat up, pushed his hat back, and quickly rose. Scooping up his rifle, he stepped to the trail to await the newcomers, who were not long in appearing.

Corncob Bob Newton and six gun sharks rounded the bend, Corncob Bob slowing when the guard lifted an arm. Their horses were caked with dust and sweat, and the men themselves showed signs of being weary after a long, hard ride. Beside Newton's horse padded Fang and Slash. "Howdy, Eb," Corncob Bob said, drawing rein. "Pike up to the house?"

"Last I saw," the guard responded, studying the gun hands with the trader. "Brought us some new blood, I take it?"

"A new bunch just in from Salt Lake City," Corncob Bob confirmed. "All hungry for money, and they don't give a hoot how they earn it." He surveyed the fields. "From the look of things, by the end of the season Pike will have enough food stored to feed an army."

"Any word from California?" asked Eb.

"About a buyer for the Injun women? No, not yet. But it shouldn't be long." Corncob Bob stared at the girl pulling weeds. "I wouldn't mind buying one myself. That gal I had ran off with that Fargo feller." Newton wiped a sleeve across his brow. "I hear tell that Pike caught him, by the way."

Eb nodded. "Caught 'im and lost 'im. Fargo got away slick as a whistle, and Pike has been spitting nails ever since. I tell you, I ain't never seen Pike so upset. He cusses the boys out for no reason at all, and gets riled over trifles."

"Wonderful," Newton muttered. "And I have to be the bearer of bad tidings."

"How's that?"

"Williams is long overdue with more building supplies." Corncob Bob swore. "You know how much Pike relies on him for seeing all the construction is done right. Why, if it weren't for Williams, that mansion would never have turned out half as nice as it did. He's the only one of us who ever worked at building things."

Eb rested the stock of his rifle on the ground. "Glad it's you who has to break the bad news and not me. Pike is liable to hit the roof. He's real anxious to get that storage building done by the end of the month."

"Is that so? Then why isn't the timber crew working?"

"They are," Eb said. "I saw Stanley takin' the bucks out at dawn."

Corncob Bob scratched his chin. "That's strange. They weren't clearing trees when we went by. Fact is, I didn't see hide nor hair of them." He shrugged. "Maybe they're working a new area."

"Nope. Stan told me it would be another couple of weeks before the crew moved farther north along the river, where some prime wood is to be had. Those were his exact words."

The trader turned his mount and pursed his lips. "It's probably nothing. But I reckon I'll go back and check it out. With someone like the Trailsman on the loose, it wouldn't pay to take anything for granted."

"Hell. He's only one man."

"Who can sling lead with the best of them," Corncob Bob responded. "They say he's half Injun, that he can track like an Apache and ride like a Comanche. A trapper I met once claimed Fargo is like a ghost in the woods. Told me he comes and goes like the wind."

Eb snickered. "Tall tales, just like they tell about Bowie and Bridger and Carson." He sniffed in disdain. "The high-and-mighty Trailsman don't scare me none. I've fought the Kiowa and the Cheyenne. If he ever tries sneakin' up on me, I'll carve him like I would a Thanksgiving turkey."

"There's such a thing as being too confident for your own good." Corncob Bob remarked, then clucked to his steed and led the half-dozen weary gun sharks back the way they had come.

Eb watched until the dust settled. Chuckling at some private joke, he strolled to the border of the cornfield and observed the women. His gaze roamed back and forth, passing over Fargo on four occasions. Each time, Fargo braced for an outcry, his hand on his pistol. But the broad blades screened him.

Eb bent to break off a piece of grass. Placing the stem between his teeth, he ambled southward, admiring the pillowy clouds.

Fargo did not waste another moment. He calculated that it would take Newton a couple of minutes to reach the clearing, another three or four to scour it and find evidence of a struggle, then about the same amount of time to locate the wagon and the bodies. Factor in yet another two for Newton and the gunmen to race to the fields, and that allowed ten to twelve minutes, total, to free the women and escape.

Fargo was none too pleased. It wasn't much, considering that Eb was now wide awake and moving away from him. He went faster, ducking under leaves, weaving around stalks, always placing each boot down with consummate care. Suddenly the teenaged girl whistled softly, just loud enough for him to hear.

The other two guards were walking briskly toward Eb, no doubt to find out what Corncob Bob had to say.

Fargo happened to be smack in between. He hugged the dank earth and pressed flush against the corn, hoping his brown buckskins would blend into the brown background of the tilled soil. He could see one of the guards, who would go by within fifteen feet of where he lay, but not the other.

Then the tramp of plodding feet told Fargo that the second man was much closer. Out of the corner of an eye he glimpsed a burly form in a plaid store-bought shirt and a craggy face covered with gristle. The man was going to walk right by him! He was bound to be seen.

"Eb! Hold up!"

Fargo saw the soles of the gunman's boots smack the ground, saw puffs of dust swirl. Peeking between two wide blades, he noted that the cutthroat held his rifle pointed down and did not have a hand on the hammer or trigger. Child's play, he reflected, bunching his knees to spring.

That was when the gunman's dark, beady eyes swung toward the stalks shielding him. Recognition and astonishment delayed the man's reaction, and in that twinkling of a second Fargo shoved to his feet and pounced. He sheared the knife in low and straight. A grunt was wrenched from the craggy mouth when the blade bit deep, and the gunman opened wider to shout.

Clamping a hand over it, Fargo sought to smother any outcry. He failed. The man's teeth sank into his palm and he had to snatch his hand back or lose part of it. Yanking the knife out, he buried the blade again, higher up.

The hardcase screeched like a woman in labor as he spiraled into a fetal curl. Instantly, Eb and the other man whirled, the latter man raising his rifle and taking deliberate aim. Before he could fire, though a pair of bronzed avengers sprang out of thin air and bore him down under their combined weight, their knives flashing repeatedly.

Eb cursed, pumped a couple of wild shots into the corn, and showed his true mettle by fleeing pell-mell down the trail toward the distant buildings.

Hastina, accompanied by two other warriors, reared up and started to give chase. Since their knives were no match for a rifle, and Fargo could ill afford to have one of them killed, he yelled Hastina's name. With obvious reluctance, the muscular warrior and his companions gave up the chase and hurried back.

Fargo turned to the forest and beckoned. Into the cornfield poured Winnemucca and the rest of the Chemehuevi warriors. At the sight of them, many of the women squealed for joy and yipped like serenading coyotes. Their reunion was touching, with tears and passionate embraces and loud talking. A woman as beautiful as Winnemucca ran to Hastina, threw her slim arms around his thick neck, and burst into tears.

Fargo almost hated to spoil the tender interlude. But Eb had reached three horses several hundred feet away and was swinging astride a sorrel. Raking his spurs, the gunman headed for the mansion. Soon Pike Cutler would be riding hell-bent for leather from the south with every last gunnie in his employ. And Corncob Bob and those other six vermin would be coming from the north. Leaving the Chemehuevis caught in the middle.

Sprinting to the maiden, Fargo seized her hand. "We've got to get the hell out of here," he demanded. "Have them follow me. Hurry!"

It was a plus in her favor that Winnemucca did not badger him with useless questions. Cupping a hand to her mouth, she did as he had bid her. From all directions the Paiutes hastened to comply, Hastina with an arm around the waist of his weeping mate. Many others still cried, and Fargo couldn't blame them, not after the nightmare they had endured.

Entering the trees, Fargo hurried toward the river. Winnemucca stayed close to him, urging her people on. The eleven women added to the twenty-two men made for a sizeable party. Finding a place for all of them to hide in the short amount of time they had before Pike Cutler and Corncob Bob took up their trail would be next to impossible. Nor did they have time to erase their tracks. So he was not going to bother trying.

Fargo was sick and tired of running and hiding. It has always been his habit to confront a problem head-on. So instead of fleeing, Fargo was going to do what the Chemehuevis should have done long ago. He was going to take the fight to their enemy.

13

In the hazy heat of late afternoon the mansion and the out-buildings sweltered. So did the four outlaws left behind. One was Lucius Quay, who nervously paced the porch, pausing now and again to tap his fingers against a white column. Over by the partially constructed storage building seven Chemehuevi men had been shackled, a precaution to prevent them from joining the upstarts who had risen in defiance against the bloody rule of Red Valley. Inside the mansion, eager women peered out through windows. Word had spread. All the Paiutes knew.

From under the overspreading branches of a weeping willow, Skye Fargo took note of where the gunmen were and what they were doing. Two were by the corner of the stable, staring off toward the fields. The last hardcase was on the top rail of the corral, a hand shielding his eyes from the sun. They knew, too. And they were worried.

Few events on the frontier spawned as much terror as an Indian uprising.

Fargo had seen Pike Cutler and ten gunmen thunder off down the trail a short while ago. Cutler probably figured the Paiutes would be sensible and flee to their village. The last thing he would expect them to do would be to attack the mansion itself or he would have left more men to guard it.

Turning to Winnemucca, Fargo said quietly, "Tell the warriors to move in. And remember, if any of those vultures gets off a shot, Cutler will come on the run and spoil our big surprise."

"My people understand," she assured him.

Fargo had to take her word for it. Gliding to the left along the tree line until he was near the rear of the mansion, he bolted to the closest corner. The Paiutes were to take care of the three underlings. Lucius Quay was all his. Pressing his back to the wall, he sidled toward the front. When he came to the porch, he halted and edged out far enough to see Quay at the head of the wide stone steps leading to the neatly trimmed yard.

None of the gunnies were looking toward the mansion. Keeping one eye on them and the other on Quay, Fargo flew to the first of the gleaming white columns. From there he sped to the next, and the next.

The gambler had his bowler hat off and was running a hand through his curly hair. Muttering, Quay tossed back his head, then bawled, "Anything, Ike?"

Fargo was halfway between the columns. In four long bounds he gained cover, just as the gunman perched on the top rail of the corral swiveled around. "I can't see hide nor hair of them now, Lucius. It looked to me like they met up with some other riders, then went off into the woods."

"That must have been Corncob Bob and his bunch," Quay guessed. "Eb mentioned that Newton showed up just before the attack."

Ike pointed at the open loft door halfway up on the stable. "I could see a lot better from there. Want me to?"

"Go ahead."

Ike jumped from the rail and vanished inside. Lucius Quay resumed pacing back and forth at the top of the steps. When a minute went by and the underling did not show, he stopped and bellowed, "Ike? Where in the hell did you get to?"

No answer issued from the shadowed interior of the stable. Quay jammed the bowler back on his head, then motioned at the two men guarding the shackled Chemehuevis. "One of you run on over and see what happened to him. Maybe the idiot fell climbing the ladder and broke his fool neck."

The thinner gunman jangled to the wide double doors and vanished inside. Quay impatiently tapped his toe.

When some time had gone by and neither Ike nor the other gunman reappeared, he lowered his hand to his nickel-plated revolver. "Ike? Jessup? What's happening in there?" The silence that ensued seemed to unnerve Cutler's lieutenant. Quay backed toward the front door, hollering, "Fredericks! Get up here! Something is wrong and I don't like it."

Fargo saw the last of the hardcases pivot and head for the house, only to be felled in his tracks by five buzzing shafts. Three slicked into Frederick's chest, two into his back. His bewhiskered face contorted in agony mercifully brief.

"Sweet Jesus!" Quay declared, and snatched at his six-shooter. Fargo was on him before the barrel cleared leather, jamming the barrel of his own pistol against Quay's temple. "Blink and you die."

Lucius Quay froze. "Fargo?" he exclaimed, but instead of sounding scared he sounded glad. "Don't let those heathens get their hands on me! I've seen what their kind can do! And I don't fancy being skinned alive or having my tongue cut out."

Fargo relieved the nervous cardsharp of the nickel-plated six-gun, then stepped to one side so he could see Quay's face. "Whether you live or die isn't up to me. All I'm interested in is your boss. And getting my pinto and my hardware back."

Quay licked his lips. "The stallion is safe in a stall. And the last I saw, your rifle and Colt were in the house, on a chair in the sitting room."

Moving to the steps, Fargo gestured at the woods. Into the open streamed the Chemehuevis, some going to their shackled fellows, some making for the portico, while from the stable came six more, Hastina at their head, all six holding knives that dripped red with freshly spilled blood.

Lucius Quay blanched and tried to melt into the wall. "Don't let them torture me!" he bleated. "Please! All I ask is a quick end!"

Winnemucca arrived with most of the Chemehuevis. "What now?" she inquired. "Do we lie in wait for Cutler to return?"

"First have the bodies dragged into the brush," Fargo instructed. "Have them stripped of their clothes and find three warriors who are about the same size to put the clothes on."

"It will be done." The maiden was off like a shot.

Fargo strode to the door and flung it wide. Suddenly he was caught in a flow of beaming Paiute women who rushed past him to embrace relatives and friends. Seven, eight, nine of them, each tearing at the clothes Cutler had forced them to wear. The kitchen help cast off white skirts and aprons and blouses. Maids ripped their black-and-white frilly uniforms from their backs and flung them down in disgust.

Quay had seized on the distraction to try and slip away. As he rotated, Fargo pointed the cocked pistol at his skull. "I wouldn't, were I you."

"Can't blame a gent for trying."

"Take me to the sitting room," Fargo commanded.

It was down the corridor and to the right, as lavish as all the other rooms, boasting thick carpet and furniture polished to a sparkling sheen. On an easy chair sat the Henry, the Colt, the Arkansas toothpick, and, much to Fargo's elation, his hat. He pushed Quay into a corner, then discarded the two pistols he held in favor of his own, checked that it was loaded, and twirled it into his holster. His hat was stained and battered, nothing some cleaning couldn't cure. Hiking his pants leg, he slid the toothpick into its ankle sheath. Finally, feeling whole again, he picked up the Henry and worked the lever to feed a cartridge into the chamber.

"What about me?" Lucius Quay asked. "I've done as you wanted, didn't I? I've behaved myself, haven't I? Why not just let me go? I swear I'll leave this godforsaken valley and never come back." In a low whine, he continued. "I'll turn over a new leaf. Walk on the straight and narrow from here on out. Just give me a second chance. White man to white man. What do you say?"

Even now the man's bigoted nature showed itself. "It's a little late to think of mending your ways," Fargo reminded him.

"What, then? What do you have in mind?"

"Help us turn the tables on Cutler and I'll speak to the Chemehuevis," Fargo said. "I can't make any promises, but they might spare you if you've never beat any of them or forced yourself on their women."

Relief caused Quay to giggle hysterically. "Fair enough. I never had much dealings with the bucks. As for the squaws, it would make me sick to my stomach to bed one. I never laid a finger on any of them."

"Outside," Fargo said curtly, leveling the Henry.

Most of the Chemehuevis were gathered in the yard. Husbands and wives who had long been denied contact embraced warmly, tears of joy glistening on many a cheek. The majority were smiling and at ease, thrilled their captivity was finally at an end. A festive mood was in the air.

Fargo had been afraid this would happen. They were getting ahead of themselves, putting the cart before the horse, as the old saw went. He saw Winnemucca arguing heatedly with an elder and caught her eye. She came when he beckoned. "What's going on?"

The maiden frowned in annoyance. "Some of them say there has been enough blood shed, enough killing. They want to return to our village. They think Cutler will leave us alone now that we have shown him we will fight back."

"Idiots," Fargo said under his breath. That was the trouble with those who were peaceable by nature. They wrongly believed that everyone else felt just as they did, and abhorred violence. They couldn't seem to get it through their heads that there were people who actually *liked* to hurt others. To her, he said, "Have them gather around. I have a few words to say. After I'm done, if they still want to quit, I won't try to stop them."

The Chemehuevis formed into a crescent moon in front of the portico, Hastina one of those in the forefront. Fargo deliberately gazed out over the whole bunch in outright contempt, then lit into them, Winnemucca translating as he talked.

"So some of you are dumb enough to want to take your

women and go home? You think that just because we've killed some of Pike Cutler's men he won't bother your people anymore? You expect him to sulk in his big lodge, licking his wounds? Is that it?" Fargo paused. "Go ahead, then, if that's what you really want. But keep this in mind. Quit now, and fifty winters from this day the Chemehuevis will only be a memory. Your tribe will no longer exist. It will have been wiped out."

No one spoke when Fargo stopped. He had their complete attention, and he made the most of it. "Pike Cutler is a rabid wolf on two legs. Wavako offered him the hand of friendship once, and where is your chief now? He was hung by the neck, remember? A man like Cutler can never live in peace with anyone because he is not at peace with himself." Fargo stabbed a finger at Hastina's wife. "What about your women? Did you know that Cutler plans to sell them as if they were cattle? That he wants to send them far away, where they will be forced to give their bodies to whites who will pay to bed them?"

A murmur rippled through the Paiutes, a murmur that grew rapidly louder.

Fargo had to raise his voice to be heard. "So go ahead, walk away if you want. Or quit fighting after one of you dies, as is your custom. But if you do, and I survive, then I'll be sure to spread the word how the Chemehuevis were too foolish to fight for their right to live."

Strong words, and they had an effect. Warriors and women were talking at once, and suddenly Hastina stepped onto the porch, his features set in sharp lines of boiling fury. Instead of addressing Fargo, he addressed his people. Winnemucca quietly relayed what he said.

"Our white friend speaks the truth. We are like prairie dogs, who run into their burrows at the first sign of danger and hide until it has passed. But this time the danger will not pass. The white known as Pike Cutler is like the rattlesnake that goes down into the prairie dog dens and kills them where they live. He will kill us, whether we stop fighting now or not. So I say we *must* fight! I say we must end our suffering!"

As soon as Hastina stopped, Fargo moved to the edge of the porch. "Let any man or woman who wants to quit do so now!" Inwardly he smiled when no one moved. "All right, then. Let's get set. Cutler and his boys will be back soon. We have to be ready."

It took a quarter of an hour, with Fargo chafing at the delay. The women were ushered into the mansion for their own safety and told to flee out the back if anything went wrong. Hastina and eight warriors hid in the stable. Others concealed themselves on the side of the mansion opposite the trail. Still others melted into the forest.

Fargo saw to the three who had donned the clothes of the dead guards. He had them tuck their long hair up under their hats. Through Winnemucca, he directed them to keep the brims low and their heads down when Cutler arrived. They were given rifles, but since they were averse to using them, they hid knives under their shirts and kept their own weapons close by. One climbed onto the top rail of the corral. The other two were positioned near their shackled brethren.

Fargo wanted to free the men still in chains, but Lucius Quay told him that Cutler had the only key. As for Quay himself, Fargo made him stand on the porch where approaching riders could plainly see him. Then Fargo slid behind the nearest column and trained the Henry on the gambler's chest. "Just act normal," he advised. "Try to warn them and you'll be the first to drop."

Quay took to pacing again, growing more and more restless as the minutes crawled by. He broke into a sweat and was constantly wiping his sleeve across his face.

Fargo glanced at Winnemucca, who stood just inside the front door, clutching a knife. She had wanted to stay by his side but he forbade it. The impending battle promised to be the bloodiest clash yet, and she might well be caught in the cross fire.

Now the drone of insects and the chirping of birds were the only sounds. The sun was on its downward arc and the shadows were lengthening. Fargo began to wonder if he had misjudged, if maybe the cutthroats had gone on to the

Paiute village and would not return for days. Then a cloud of dust roiled skyward out to where the fields and the forest met, and soon a knot of riders materialized. "They are coming!" Fargo had Winnemucca call out.

Pike Cutler and Corncob Bob Newton were in the lead, the two mongrels loping beside the trader's mount. Eight or nine hardcases were bunched together close behind, the rest strung out singly and in pairs. Cutler looked none too happy. When they drew within sight of the corral, the Chemehuevi on the top rail raised an arm and waved, as Fargo had directed him to. It was a nice touch, sure to lull Cutler into thinking all was well.

Lucius Quay had removed his hat and was gnawing on his lower lip. He looked at Fargo, then at the Henry, and his features clouded.

"Don't even think it," Fargo warned.

On came the fiery lord of Red Valley and his coldhearted minions. Fargo had anticipated that some would rein up at the corral, while others might come to the house with Cutler. He was taken aback when *all* of them angled toward the mansion, and saw Quay stiffen. "Act natural!" he whispered.

Pike Cutler halted a dozen feet out instead of at the hitching post. "We lost their trail at the river," he announced. "They went into the water but didn't cross. My guess is they went north, toward the mouth of the valley. We're going to pack up some grub and stay out all damn night if we have to in order to catch them." Cutler slid his right boot from the stirrup and began to dismount, then paused. "How are things here, Lucius?"

Fargo had told Quay to stand so that he could see Quay's face at all times. But abruptly, Cutler's lieutenant turned so his back was to the column.

"Just fine," Quay answered, his voice cracking slightly.

Pike Cutler straightened. "What's the matter with you? Are you ill? You're sweating as if you have a fever." He motioned at the shackled captives. "I want you to unchain those wretches so we can take them with us. When we overtake the upstarts, I'll threaten to kill them unless the others surrender."

Quay had the key all along! The realization spiked through Fargo too late. He wedged the Henry to his shoulders as all hell broke loose.

Lucius Quay sprang to the steps and screeched, "It's a trap, Pike! It's a trap!" even as Fang and Slash suddenly snarled and raced toward the two Chemehuevis who had on the clothes of the dead guards. Apparently the mongrels had caught their scent. And at that selfsame moment, one of the gunmen at the rear pointed at the warrior on the top corral rail and hollered, "Hey! That ain't Ike! It's a stinkin' Injun!"

Fargo fixed a hasty bead on Pike Cutler and squeezed the trigger. But just as he fired, Cutler wheeled his horse. The shot missed, the heavy lead slamming into a hardcase unlimbering a revolver.

His shot was the signal for the Chemehuevis. From three directions they hurtled toward their former captors. Hastina led a frenzied rush from the stable and was among the gunmen first. From around the corner of the house charged more warriors, shrieking and yipping, while from the trees hurtled the rest. Arrows whizzed in precise flight. Lances were thrown with unerring aim. And then the startled gunmen brought their pistols and rifles into play, rocking the valley with the din of booming gunfire.

Bedlam swirled in a deafening whirlwind of shooting, slashing, and hacking. It was every man for himself, white and red jumbled together, curses and screams and war whoops rising in strident chorus.

Into the melee plunged Skye Fargo. Trying to settle the sights of the Henry on one of the dodging, twisting gunmen from the porch was hopeless. He must be in the thick of it with the Chemehuevis. As he bounded from the steps to the grass, a horse and rider loomed out of the fray. A panicked gunman had spurred a roan into a gallop to flee and in his panic the man did not care if he rode anyone down.

Throwing himself to the right, Fargo fired his Henry from the hip. The slug punched the rider from the saddle, lifeless, and the roan pounded on past. Rising onto a knee, Fargo spied another gunnie about to shoot Hastina in the back. He was a shade faster, the kick of the Henry against his shoulder simultaneous with the kick of the gunnie backward.

Outlaws and warriors were locked in mortal combat, the Paiutes seeking to bury their knives, the gunmen trying to get off shots. Bodies littered the grass, some twitching, some still. As near as Fargo could tell in the frantic ebb and flow of the brutal conflict, neither side had the upper hand. But he had one thing to be thankful for. The Chemehuevis were fighting on, even though a number of them had died. Was his little speech the deciding factor? Or had they finally, fully realized that the very existence of their people was at stake?

Darting into the thick of things, Fargo fired as swiftly as targets presented themselves. He blasted another cutthroat from the saddle, winced at a stinging sensation in his shoulder, and flung lead at the hardcase who had creased him. Always in motion, always spinning and ducking and making himself as hard to hit as he could, he penetrated into the heart of the battleground where the toll was its bloodiest.

Gunsmoke hung like acrid fog over everyone and everything. Suddenly a short gunman appeared out of the soup, spied him, and fanned the hammer of a Remington four times. Fanning a pistol was a fast way to empty a cylinder, but at the critical expense of accuracy. All four shots missed.

Fargo pumped the lever of the Henry and pitched the gunman into eternity. Dirt erupting in a miniature geyser at his feet alerted him to another killer anxious to nail him. Fargo emptied the Henry into the outlaw's chest, let the Henry fall, and resorted to the Colt. Momentarily in the clear, he saw that the tide had turned in favor of Cutler's gang. Fully half the Chemehuevis were down or wounded. Knives and clubs were no match for six-shooters and rifles. In another couple of minutes it would all be over.

It was then that Fargo heard a siren shriek he could not account for, a banshee wailing that swelled in volume until it almost drowned out the gun blasts and the frenzied uproar. It took a few moments for the source to register. Whirling, Fargo saw the women stream from the mansion. They held knives, brooms, busted pieces of furniture, anything and everything that could be used as a weapon. Into the fracas they hurled themselves, two or three women going after each gunman. They stabbed, ripped, and clawed with their nails. They bit, kicked, and gouged. In a fierce wave they engulfed the outlaws and vented the pent-up rage they had long held in check. The killers did not stand a prayer.

Fargo pivoted again, and there was Lucius Quay not ten feet away, a smoking revolver in his hand. Both of them brought their pistols up. Fargo's cracked a split instant sooner but Quay's still went off, a lethal hornet buzzing past Fargo's ear. His own shot cored Quay's cheek and burst out the rear of Quay's skull.

A bellow more beastlike than human drew Fargo's gaze to the cause of all the carnage. Pike Cutler was on foot, desperately bowling over warriors and women alike as he barged toward the mansion. His once-fine clothes were a shambles, torn and rent and smeared with blood and gore. He broke free and sped up the steps, pausing to snap a shot at a warrior who had given chase. Then he dashed through the doorway.

Fargo raced past the dazed Chemehuevis, past the prone body. Leaping onto the porch, he ran to the entrance but stopped shy of it. A prudent precaution, for when he leaned forward to see down the hall a revolver cracked and a bullet bit into the jamb. Backpedaling to the first window, Fargo pried at the sill. It opened readily, and with a hop he was over and in.

The house was eerily still. Outside, the fight raged but the sounds were muffled. Fargo crossed to the door, which hung open, and peeked out. The corridor was empty. His back flush to the wall, he slid from the room and crept forward. He came abreast of the stairs that wound to the second floor and heard a rumbling voice above, drawing closer.

"—stop the heathens yet! The miserable scum!"

Pike Cutler stomped onto the landing and started down. At the sight of Fargo, he stopped. "You!" he snarled, hefting a wooden keg clasped in his enormous paws. "It's all your doing. When I'm done with those savages, I'll deal with you." His features were a twisted perversion of anything human, his eyes wide, the pupils dilated. "This will do the job!" He lifted the keg higher, revealing a fuse that jutted from the top.

Fargo's Colt boomed twice.

Jarred onto his heels, Pike Cutler swayed but did not fall. Hissing defiantly, his left hand moved and a match flared bright. "Think that will stop *me*?" he railed.

Again Fargo worked the hammer, and a third time. Each shot staggered the man mountain. Yet Cutler's iron will propelled him down the stairs, one lumbering step at a time. The match touched the tip of the fuse, which spit sparks and hissed like a venomous serpent. Spinning, Fargo sprinted toward the entrance.

Mocking laughter echoed off the walls. Mad peals of mirth that followed Fargo through the doorway and onto the porch. Winnemucca, Hastina, and several other Chemehuevis were coming up the steps, and he waved them back, yelling, "Run! Run for your lives!" His tone and his gestures were enough to spur them into flight, and they spilled onto the grass. Fargo grabbed the maiden's wrist, then veered toward the stable. They never made it.

A tremendous concussion rent the air, and they were buffeted as if by an unseen fist. Fargo stumbled, glancing back as he sprawled onto his knees bearing Winnemucca with him. The outer wall of the mansion exploded outward, all that glass and wood shattered into ruin as a fireball of immense proportions expanded with the speed of thought. Columns cracked and caved in. The porch heaved upward in a paroxysm of destruction.

Fargo fell across the maiden, protecting her with his own body. A wave of heat blistered them. Then debris began to rain down in a steady shower of bits and pieces, some small but others large enough to crush them to a pulp. A section of wall larger than the Ovaro thudded into the earth yards away. Chemehuevis screamed in terror, wailed in torment.

The mansion's roof gave way. Rending and cracking sounds heralded its collapse, and as the heavy timbers crashed down they brought more of the walls toppling with them. Flames licked hungrily at the rubble, devouring the monument to one man's inflated sense of his own self-importance.

Fargo slowly stood, helping Winnemucca to rise. He scanned the battleground. All around them shocked Chemehuevis gaped or spoke in awed whispers. Bodies were everywhere, white and red alike. A few horses had also been felled by random shots, and on the other side of the yard lay the scarlet-flecked bodies of the two vicious mongrels, side by side.

"Is it over?" Winnemucca asked in stunned disbelief. "Is it really, truly over?"

"Yes," Skye Fargo said, draping an arm around her shoulders. He would stay on for a day or two to help her people, and then it was off to the Bear River country.

"Hold me."

"Gladly." Fargo hugged the maiden close, feeling her ample bosom rub his chest and the warmth of her lush body through the dress. Maybe he would stay on for three or four days, instead.

LOOKING FORWARD!
The following is the opening
section from the next novel in the exciting
Trailsman series from Signet:

**THE TRAILSMAN #198
BLACKGULCH GAMBLE**

*1860, in a Texas town called Blackgulch,
a man could find any crooked game
he wanted to play if he was willing to stake
his gold, his woman, and his life . . .*

"Lay down your bets, men! Three to one on the big red,
three to one, now lay your bets!" A squat man in a green
hat was moving through the crowd. "He's a champeen, that
big red. Going to be a bloody fight. Bloody, bloody fight to
the finish! Three to one!"

The tall stranger with the dark beard paused and looked
over the heads of the roiling throng gathered at dusk around
a small fenced enclosure in the middle of the dockside
street in New Orleans. Two men, each clutching a struggling rooster, eyed each other warily. The cocks' heads
moved convulsively back and forth, their ruddy combs
trembling, their beady eyes black. Around the birds' yellow
legs were strapped razor-sharp spurs. Onlookers tossed
coins and dollar bills into a box.

"Three to one, three to one on the big red! A real champeen, one of the best! Get ready!" The green-hatted man shouldered his way toward the tall, quiet stranger. "How about you, mister? Three to one! Take it from me and put it on the big red. Sure to win. Make you some fast bucks."

"Don't care for cockfights," the tall man mumbled as he pushed his way out of the crowd. His lake blue eyes scanned the New Orleans street. Along the row of brick buildings with lacy wrought-iron porches and stairways, street lamps were being lit, golden flames sparkling in the glass globes. The sky above still held the light of sunset. The street was jammed with a restless moving horde that rushed and eddied like a tumultuous river.

The cacophony of voices, of shouts and cries, was deafening. A roar welled up as the cockfight began, and the crows pressed against him, trying to get closer to the excitement. Off to his left, a dour fellow sat on the seat of a shebang and called out the prices of patent medicines. A thimble rigger tried to get suckers to put down quarters as he deftly moved small thimbles across a felt-covered table, lifting one from time to time to show the joker, a little white pebble, underneath. Another man called out an advertisement for new boots while a rotund woman offered glasses of draft beer from the back of a wagon for twenty cents a mug. A band of street musicians stood on a wrought-iron porch and played trumpets, drums, and flutes, but he could only catch an occasional strain of melody amidst all the ruckus.

New Orleans was a jumbalaya stew of every kind of person imaginable, Skye Fargo thought to himself. A swarthy couple passed by, their dark wavy hair and colorfully ribboned clothes marking them as Creole. There were mulattoes from Jamaica, a German fellow in a feather hat, a couple of pretty Italian women, a Cockney fresh from St. Giles from the sound of his accent.

The wild and steamy city of New Orleans was a crossroads. From here a man traveled across the gulf to the southern islands or out across the vast expanse of land toward the western frontier or northward up the broad highway of the river.

Beyond the crowd, Fargo glimpsed the muddy brown Mississippi, wide as a lake and seemingly motionless. A flock of ships anchored just offshore waved high masts against the peach-blow clouds, like a forest of swaying trees. A long dock jutted out into the water. He looked up the river but saw no sign of the paddleboat *Lady Luck*. When would it arrive? The sunset was just fading. Maybe another hour, he thought. Around about nightfall, they had said. He'd just finished a job and had a big wad of cash pushed deep into an inner pocket of his jacket. He could use a rest, he'd decided. A hot bath every day, good food, fine brandy, some female company. So he'd decided a week on a gambling riverboat paddling up the Mississippi would cure him of his itch for the comforts of civilization. For a while anyway. And the *Lady Luck* was reputed to be one of the most luxurious riverboats on the river.

Fargo spotted a gleaming white standing-top phaeton drawn by two snowy horses and driven by an old man in a frock coat. The open carriage was inching through the packed street. But what attracted his attention was the woman who sat inside. Her gleaming dark hair was piled high, stuck with a red ostrich feather that fluttered each time she turned her head. Below her jewel-wound neck her scarlet gown was cut daringly low to reveal mounds of generous breasts and deep cleavage. She seemed to be looking for something out on the river. He pushed his way through the mob until he was within ten feet of her. She happened to glance back and catch his gaze.

Her eyes were the startling color of cornflowers, almost pale purple, fringed with thick dark lashes, punctuated by dramatically arched brows. For all the sophistication of her dress, there seemed to be a kind of innocence in her eyes, almost a naive surprise. She smiled, rose-dimpled, as her eyes held his for a brief moment. Then she tugged the driver's coat. He halted and she rose to get out of the carriage.

Fargo elbowed his way toward her and offered his hand. She took it and stepped out. She was short, just reaching his broad chest. He bent down slightly and put his lips to her ear. The din was so loud, he practically had to shout.

"You looking for the *Lady Luck* too?"

She seemed surprised at the question and pulled back, looking at him suspiciously. She nodded hesitantly.

"I figured as much. I saw you looking toward the river," he explained. "I'm waiting for the same riverboat."

Her lips formed a silent *Oh* and she nodded. He started to ask her name, but she swiftly raised one hand as if bidding him good-bye.

"I suppose I'll see you on board," she called out stiffly and turned her back, making her way through the crowd.

Fargo swore to himself and watched her go. There was no understanding women. He watched other men turn to admire her as she slipped among them. She'd hardly got five yards through the throng when three Aussies bumped into her. They were an unsavory lot, unshaven and mean-looking. He'd noticed them before—they sure looked like ex-convicts. And now they'd noticed the woman in red and saw she was unaccompanied.

Although he couldn't hear their words over the hubbub, Fargo could imagine what the three men were saying as they suddenly surrounded her. She turned about in a swirl of crimson, her expression puzzled, then angry, then frightened. He could tell, even through the crowd, the men were making a grab for her. Fargo shoved his way toward them, closer and closer. They had her surrounded and were hustling her toward a dark alley. She was struggling, her mouth open in a scream, but in the blaring commotion she couldn't be heard. No one was taking notice.

In a few swift strides Fargo caught up to them, reached out a strong arm, and grabbed a collar, suddenly hauling one of the men backward. The man lost his balance and whirled about, surprise on his grizzled face. Fargo swung a whistling left that snapped his head half around, and the man's eyes rolled back as he crumpled into a heap. The crowd eddied around them. The second man, tall and broad, pushed the woman behind him and brought up his fists. Fargo lashed out again, but the man stepped backward, then struck, a stinging right to Fargo's belly. Fargo swore at the pain and ducked a sizzling left that whistled through the air, then balled his rock-hard fist and drove it upward into the tall man's jaw. His head snapped back—just as Fargo felt a kick against his leg that barely missed his groin. The third man, short and stocky, had come about. The tall man was staggering, and Fargo followed with another drive, a powerful left into his midsection. The tall man gasped for air like a fish, and his knees gave way. Just then Fargo felt an electric shock along his jaw, followed by dancing stars, and the crowd scene began to whirl. The third man had delivered a near-knockout punch. Fargo gritted his teeth. The short man's face swam in front of his eyes as if in a dream, and the man's fist was heading toward his face. With a shout of rage, Fargo pulled up his fists in a lightning-fast motion, blocked the punch, and drove hard, smashing once, twice, a third time into the short man's head.

In a moment it was over, and the last man went down. Fargo took a deep breath and shook his head to clear it. Rubbing his face, he felt the bruise and swelling along the jaw. Nothing broken. He looked around for the woman in red, expecting to see her there. He turned, looked behind him, scanned the swirling crowd. But she was gone. Well, that figured.

He moved away from the spot before the three troublemakers could come to their senses. The sunset had faded completely, the evening stars were out, and the golden-flamed lamps glimmered in the blue dusk all along the crowded street. Fargo pushed his way toward the side street that led to the stables where he'd left the Ovaro. He might as well fetch the pinto down to the dock, ready to board, since the *Lady Luck* would be coming along any time now. He'd reserved the best stateroom on board and made arrangements for the pinto to be transported on deck. Yeah, he was looking forward to this trip.

As he rounded the corner, he came to a narrow alley behind the stables and noticed a rear door. It was ajar and he walked in. The warm odor of hay and animals enveloped him. Inside it was dark with only one oil lamp lit in the distance, at the main entrance. He heard men's voices, at least a dozen, but couldn't quite make out the words. He started to walk forward, then something in their tone—an urgency, a secrecy—made him stop, melt into the shadow along the line of stalls and ease forward until he could make out what they were saying.

"So, did you even spot her?" one said.

"In that crowd? You gotta be kidding." It was a gravelly voice, low and distinctive.

"Well, we know she always wears red. That should make it easy."

"Yeah, real easy. There's a thousand women out there in red dresses tonight. I told you this was a harebrained idea."

Fargo crept closer until he was just at the edge of the light. At least a dozen men, maybe more, stood by the open doors. It was too dark to see any faces.

"All right, all right. Keep your shirt on."

"Even if we see her, we're not going to be able to do anything." It was the gravel-voiced one again. "So what if we find her? What are we going to do about it? Grab her right in the middle of the street? There's a thousand people around all the time."

"All right, all right. At least we found out she's traveling on the *Lady Luck*. That's all we need. There's nothing more we can do here. Let's go catch up with the others."

Fargo stood motionless against the stall as the shadowy men saddled up and led their horses from the stable. He heard the creak of leather as they mounted, the clop of hooves on cobblestones as they rode away. He waited until the last sound faded. Then he went to the Ovaro's stall. The black and white pinto nuzzled him. He lit a lamp and began saddling the horse. All the while he was preoccupied by what the mysterious men had said. Were they talking about the same woman in red? He didn't like what he'd heard. It sounded like she was heading for trouble. Big trouble. He was leading the Ovaro out the front door and into the street when he heard the crackle of footsteps. The hunchbacked stable master was hobbling toward him as fast as he could.

"Hold up, Mr. Fargo!" the old man panted. He paused and held onto the side of the pinto's saddle as he gasped and caught his breath. "Got a message for you. Must be important. I said I'd get it to you for sure."

The old man pulled an envelope out of his jacket and handed it over. Fargo moved toward the oil lamp and turned it over in his hands. The thick envelope was postmarked Arizona a few weeks ago. He'd been in Arizona about a month before.

"It must be real important," the old man repeated. "The man who delivered it said they've been trying to track you down for a long, long time."

Fargo tore open the envelope, but instead of a message, he found another envelope inside. This was postmarked Nevada. Yeah, he'd been there recently too. The third envelope was from Wyoming and the fourth from Montana. Whatever the message was, it had been trailing him for a while but never quite caught up. Finally, inside the last envelope he found the message, a telegram that had been sent to Denver City from Blackgulch three months before. And that was all that was clear. The rest was a bunch of meaningless letters bunched together. Unreadable. Someone had written across it "Garbled in transmission. Correction requested but no reply. Denver City Telegraph Office."

The old man was looking over his arm, trying to read the message.

"Looks like some kind of code," the stablemaster said, impressed.

"Nah, it's just a mess," Fargo said. Great. There was no way to tell what the message was supposed to say. He didn't have a clue who had sent it. He examined it again. *Blackgulch*. That was the one word he could read. But Blackgulch where? He shook his head. There were probably a dozen rinky-dink towns called Blackgulch out in the western territories. There was no telling where the message had come from. Whoever sent it had probably given up on him by now—three months was a long time. He folded up the message along with the envelopes and tucked them in his inside vest pocket, bid the stablemaster good-bye, and led the pinto away.

As he turned onto the thronged dockside street, out on the river he spotted the glistening ivory boat called the *Lady Luck*. She was a beautiful sight, steaming straight toward the dock. Her wide white bow was reflected on the muddy water like a grand lady with a hoop skirt gliding across a polished ballroom floor. Her two smokestacks puffed gray clouds against the stars, the paddle slapped the river, and the three gingerbread balconies sparkled with golden torches. Across the water he could hear strains of music and the vivacious laughter of the men and women onboard. Fargo led the pinto out onto the long wooden dock.

The woman in red stood looking out at the approaching riverboat. Beside her loomed a small mountain of red leather luggage. Fargo walked up beside her and touched the brim of his hat as her wide cornflower eyes blinked up at him, startled.

"Oh. Oh—you again," she said. Her black eyebrows arched, and she turned her attention to the oncoming *Lady Luck*.

"Pretty cool welcome to someone who got those three bruisers off you," he said, feeling a bit hot under the collar.

She looked up at him again, and her expression softened. "Forgive me," she said with a smile. "I'm being thoughtless. Of course. Thank you for what you did back there. Forgive me?" She laid a light hand on his arm. Her lashes were dark and long, fringes around her eyes. Those eyes. Just how innocent was she? Never mind. She was beautiful anyway. He grinned down at her and introduced himself.

"And I'm Ruby Murphy." She offered her hand.

"Got some bad news for you," he said. And he told her about what he'd overheard in the stables. When he'd finished she burst into a merry laugh.

"But that's absurd! I have no idea who those men were. They must have been talking about somebody else. Nobody's coming after me. The whole thing's ridiculous!"

"You can't think of anybody who might be looking for you?"

"Not a soul!" Ruby said without hesitation.

"Well, you ought to watch out anyhow."

"Or have somebody watch out for me, I bet you mean." Ruby glanced at him out of the corners of her eyes. "Why, Mr. Fargo I've rarely heard a man make up such a foolish story just to try to scare a woman into thinking she needs his protection. Nobody is looking for me. Except maybe you, of course. And I am perfectly able to take care of myself."

"I'll remember that next time I see three men try to drag you off," he said. He'd had enough. Ruby Murphy was beautiful, but she was also too difficult and stubborn. If she wasn't going to take his advice, then to hell with her. He turned away and led the pinto to a point close to the boarding ramp. He could feel her eyes on him, but he'd be damned if he'd look back. Instead, he turned his attention to the several horses waiting to be boarded. A spectacular Arabian horse stood nearby. It was one of the finest mounts he'd seen—after the Ovaro, of course. The Arabian's long legs and slender neck marked it as a thoroughbred with a lot of speed, but it also had the powerful chest and strong haunches that would make it a steed with great endurance.

The man holding the Arabian's bridle was smallish, wiry. He was dressed in a walnut homespun shirt, stained leather breeches, and battered boots that had seen better days. The man noticed Fargo's attention and doffed his hickory slouch hat. Everything about him was brown—his thick, ragged-cut hair, his crookedly trimmed mustache, his worn complexion. He looked like a country rube, the kind of man who made his way by taking on odd jobs and doing some trapping and trading. An unusual owner for such an expensive horse.

"Fine horse," Fargo said appreciatively.

"Yours too," the man responded with a friendly smile as he eyed the black and white pinto.

"Don't see many Arabians around. Must have cost a pretty penny."

"Didn't cost a nickel," the man in brown responded with a laugh as if abashed. "I just got lucky in a coin toss one day. The name's Josh Leatherberry."

"Skye Fargo."

"Why, you're the one folks call the Trailsman," Leatherberry said, his face wrinkling with surprise. "Well, I'm sure glad to meet you."

"So you won that horse with a coin toss? You always have that kind of luck?"

"Hell, no," Leatherberry said, his face open and bemused. "I'd say till I won this horse, I'd never been lucky in my life. Just a hardworking man trying to get by. Anyhow, Mr. Fargo," he went on as if eager to change the subject, "I've heard a lot about you over the years, and I'm glad to finally meet you." Leatherberry stuck out his hand.

As they shook, Fargo felt a wave of surprise. Josh Leatherberry's hand was as soft and narrow as a woman's, his fingers smooth as silk with nary a callus. Hardly the kind of hands Fargo had expected on such a rough-looking man. Nevertheless, he kept the surprise off his face. There was obviously more to Josh Leatherberry than first met the eye.

Just then, with a jolt and a scraping of wood on wood, the *Lady Luck* pulled up alongside the dock. Three men jumped off and made her fast with ropes as the gangplank was lowered. Women in bright colors and gambling men in their brocade vests and waxed mustaches began to disembark. After a few minutes, the passengers were all off and the trunks and crates unloaded. A crowd of travelers had gathered, waiting to get onboard. Fargo saw an elderly black man with silvery hair standing at the top of the gangplank.

"All aboard!" he called out. "*Lady Luck* now boarding passengers for the trip to St. Louie. All aboard!"

The woman in red swept up the gangplank first, her tall ostrich feather fluttering. A couple of crew members scurried behind carrying her red leather bags. A swarm of other travelers, professional gamblers and their doves by the looks of them, followed.

"You down there! You with the horses!" the black man was calling out. "Get ready to board."

"Why are you going up to St. Louie?" Fargo asked casually as he and Leatherberry brought their steeds toward the gangplank. He was more and more curious about the strange man in brown with the Arabian horse.

"Oh, I never been on a gamblin' boat before," Leatherberry said with a shrug. "But when I won this here Araby horse, I thought maybe luck was running with me. Don't really know anything about cards and all. But this past winter I made a good piece of money trapping some beaver, and I thought I'd put it down on the tables and see if my luck would stay with me."

Fargo nodded affably, thinking the man's smooth hands had not recently—if ever—tied a buckskin thong on a trap, or hacked through ice with a broad ax, or scraped flesh off beaverskin. Josh Leatherberry was telling a lie for sure. He was no more a trapper than he was a dance-hall girl. Well, whatever Leatherberry's story really was, he was a man to keep an eye on. He felt curiosity prick him. But, he told himself, for one whole week he was just going to relax and enjoy himself.

He led the Ovaro clopping up the gangplank, and Leatherberry followed with the Arabian. At the top they were met by the elderly black man.

"I'm Sims, steward of the *Lady Luck*," the man said, his brown eyes flashing. He consulted a piece of paper in his hand. "You gentlemen must be Mr. Fargo and Mr. Leatherberry. Now, just bring your horses this way."

Sims led the way along the deck toward the rear, where a small wooden shelter stood back by the paddle wheel. Inside were several stalls filled with hay. Fargo made sure the Ovaro would have plenty of feed and water.

"Now, Mr. Fargo, I'll take you to your stateroom," Sims said. "You'll be staying in the presidential suite. And Mr. Leatherberry, I see that you've booked passage to sleep on deck."

Leatherberry, busy unsaddling the Arabian, nodded.

"Some of us got to save money and ain't quite so fancy," he said with a grin at Fargo. There was no envy or malice in it, and Fargo found himself liking Josh Leatherberry, despite the air of mystery around his circumstances.

"See you around," Fargo said and followed Sims.

They walked along the wide-planked deck, and Sims paused in front of a gleaming mahogany door with a brass sign, *Number One*. The room inside was worthy of the finest hotel. It was paneled in dark rich wood with sparkling brass fittings. A big brass bed stood in the center, and the wide bay windows showed a view of the broad river and the distant bank. The adjoining room held a large copper bathing tub.

"Dinner is served at six o'clock. Meanwhile, you just

ring me if you want some hot water or anything else, sir," Sims said as he departed.

Fargo lay down on the wide bed and closed his eyes. Yeah, this was the life. A week of rest and good food, a hot bath every day, gambling, and some female company—he thought of the woman in red and wondered where she was staying. He felt the *Lady Luck* bobbing in the water, then heard the paddle wheel begin to churn. With a bump and a scrape the huge riverboat swung out into the current and gently rocked back and forth as it began its journey north. He let himself be lulled to sleep.